Love Under Suspicion
Swimming Kangaroo Books, April 2006

Swimming Kangaroo Books
Arlington, Texas

ISBN: 1-934041-02-5

This book is a work of fiction and any resemblance to persons, living or dead, or events is purely coincidental. They are productions of the author's imagination and used fictitiously. While the Texas setting of the book is real, specific locations are fictional or are used in a fictional sense and are in now way intended to depict actual events.

Cover art by Kelly Carter

Swimming
Kangaroo
Books

CHAPTER ONE

Dear Abby,

How have you been? Things are going pretty well here, in fact, there's a chance I may be out as early as next week. Early release for good behavior. Ha! Ha!

The grapevine has it that you've been keeping the family business alive and thriving. I'm looking forward to coming home and seeing what you've done. Also hear you've kept up with our old contacts and acquired some new ones. I knew I could count on you. Hope there will be a place for me in your new scheme of things.

Ever lovingly yours,
Joe

Sloane Jameson read the letter with barely a flicker

of his cobalt blue eyes and slid it across the table to Connie. She picked it up with manicured fingertips and scanned the lines, her eyes snapping with lively interest. Then she handed the letter back to their supervisor.

"Well?" The supervisor invited comment.

"Suggestive, isn't it?" Sloane looked questioningly at Connie.

Connie pursed her lips, today painted a fire engine red. "I presume we've investigated her."

The supervisor tapped a folder at her elbow. "As you can see, her file is this thick. There's nothing we could really call evidence, but there's plenty of cause for suspicion."

Sloane pulled the folder over to himself and studied the cover photo. A fine-boned woman with reddish-blonde hair and sparkling green eyes smiled out at him, a wholesome-looking, girl-next-door type. The last person in the world you would expect to be involved with drugs. Sloane opened the folder and rifled through the sheath of papers inside. Then he shoved the folder back to his supervisor and cleared his throat. "Joe Tarleton is getting out?" There was a brittle component to his voice.

The supervisor looked pained. "Yes. Apparently he's been a model prisoner, and what with overcrowding..." She spread her arms wide in a gesture of helplessness. "That is why you two are here."

"Yes?" Connie leaned forward, her eyes narrowing with interest.

"This may be our chance to get to the man in charge."

"Of the entire drug ring?" Sloane's voice had an edge on it. "We know that the drug ring Tarleton worked for supplies drugs all over Texas and the southwest, but we've never been able to pick up anybody but some two-bit dealers. Joe has been our biggest catch to date, and we believe that once he is released, he will return to his involvement with the gang."

"So you want us to trail Joe Tarleton?" Connie asked slowly.

"Not exactly. We'll put someone else on that. We want you to carry out a surveillance on his wife."

"His wife?" Sloane's eyes returned to the photo of Abby Tarleton.

"Actually his ex-wife," the supervisor allowed. "She divorced him soon after the trial. But our reports from prison indicate that Tarleton is still in love with his wife and plans to return to her when he is released. When he does, I want you two to already be in place. Your mission will be two-fold. First, you are to get any information you can about the leaders of this drug ring. And second, if there's any proof that Abby Tarleton is involved, you are to get it so we can nail her. So far she's managed to elude us. I want that to end with you two." The supervisor issued Connie and Sloane a challenging look.

Sloane and Connie took a long look at each other and then nodded. "Understood," they said simultaneously.

Abby Tarleton hung up the phone, nibbling discontentedly on her lower lip. For a moment she stared sightlessly out the kitchen window. Perhaps she should have told Ned no, he couldn't come over. Not now, not ever again. She didn't want him around, didn't want the contact with his friends, the constant reminders of a time of her life that she would just as soon forget. Drumming her long fingertips on the butcher-block table, Abby sighed. Whether she liked it or not, Ned was family, even if he was just her stepbrother. Family helped family when they were in trouble. He had helped her out years before, after her husband's arrest for drug dealing.

Shaking her head, Abby reflected wryly, "Yeah,

and I've been repaying that debt ever since." She glanced at her son's bedroom door. He was starting to stir, but she ought to have just enough time to give the other side of the duplex a final inspection before the new tenants arrived. She stood up slowly and slipped outside to go next door.

As she stepped out, she braced herself against the onslaught of the Texas heat that was always a shock after being in the air-conditioned indoors. Squinting her eyes against the afternoon sun, she glanced across the street and froze, a cold chill gripping her despite the ninety-eight-degree weather.

The old red Nova was still there, its driver obscured by a newspaper, the license plate muddied beyond readability. He had been parked there for the past three weeks, and off and on, Abby had the impression that he was peering at her over the top of his paper. Once he had even followed her to the airport, but had dropped the tail as soon as she had driven through the gates. Abby stared at him, trying to discern any recognizable features, but his face remained well hidden. She wondered if she should call the police, but with a sigh, decided against it. He hadn't actually done anything, and as far as she knew, there was no law against parking in a public street.

Puffing out her cheeks with an exhaled breath, she crossed the yard and entered the other side of the duplex. As she moved through the empty rooms, she critically examined every nook and cranny, opening doors and drawers and running her fingers over the moldings. She drew on the memory of the much dreaded military housing inspections her mother had gone through each of the many times her army father had changed stations. The military inspectors were notorious for nitpicking, yet Abby knew that this side of the duplex would have no trouble passing a military inspection.

The duplex was an empty duplicate of the half she lived in. She had bought it just before Adam was born, after her husband's arrest. Between the rent from the duplex and her tiny airfreight business, she was able to keep her head above water and the wolf from her door.

Abby ran her fingers through her reddish-blonde hair. Her blood still did a slow boil when she thought of how Joe had deceived her, although even after she had learned the truth, she had acted the part of a good little wife and stood by him. She'd hired the best lawyers, unflinchingly put up bail money, and sat tirelessly in court under the misguided belief that one didn't kick a man when he was down. Only after Joe had been convicted and sentenced to prison had she filed for divorce. She looked at it as coming to her senses, although she knew Joe and Ned saw it as abandonment.

Never one to do things halfway, once Abby had decided to put Joe out of her life, she did it completely. She sold their house and furniture and used the money to purchase the duplex. Except for a formal note when Adam had been born, she did not communicate with Joe, and refused to open or acknowledge any of his letters. She immersed herself in her son and her business, and at twenty-eight, felt satisfied with her life the way it was.

Now she looked critically at the empty duplex. Cream-colored walls surrounded the brown-carpeted floors in the living room, while the surprisingly large kitchen sported blue and white checkerboard tile on the floor and white Formica countertops.

Abby mentally reviewed the state of her finances. Hopefully when these tenants moved out, barring unforeseen catastrophes, she should have enough to repaint both sides of the duplex. At last. satisfied that everything was clean and ready for her new tenants, she went back to her side of the duplex. Airplane noises came from Adam's bedroom. She poked her head around the door, and he gave her a cheery smile that lifted her heart. He was the one good thing that had come from her ill-fated marriage

"Ready to get up, Adam?" Abby held out her hand.

Adam hopped out of his airplane bed that he had just received for his third birthday, replacing the battered old crib he'd slept in since birth. "Cookies?" he asked hopefully.

"Graham crackers. And juice," Abby said firmly. "Come on. Let's get you cleaned up before the new tenants arrive."

She had just finished tidying up after Adam's snack when the doorbell rang. Abby flung the dishtowel over a chair and grabbed Adam's sturdy hand. "Come on, Tiger. Let's go play landlord."

She opened the door, a ready smile on her face. "Hi," she said. "I'm Abby Tarleton." Her voice trailed off uncertainly. Standing before her, tall and straight like a towering spruce, was the sexiest man she'd seen in a long time. His black, unruly hair fell casually across his forehead, and the blue of his eyes was like a cold wave.

"I'm Sloane Jameson," he said with a deep timbered voice. "I believe you've met my wife, Connie." His flesh met Abby's in a warm clasp.

Abby hastily drew her hand away, shaken by her response to the brief contact. "Yes, of course." She turned to his wife, resolving not to look at him any more than was necessary. "Nice to see you again, Mrs. Jameson." Her voice stayed low and calm, giving no hint of her inner turmoil.

"Thank you. My husband and I are eager to get moved in as quickly as possible." There was just a tinge of frost in Connie Jameson's voice, which wasn't surprising, Abby told herself, since her new landlady was busy making eyes at her husband.

Abby dug into her pocket and pulled out a key ring. With an unfamiliar spurt of self-consciousness, she found herself wishing she'd dressed up a little. Suddenly her faded cut-offs and tattered tank shirt seemed woefully shabby next to Connie Jameson's perfectly coifed look. Even in the stifling heat, Connie seemed cool and crisp in a business-like suit, stockings, heels, and beauty parlor hair. Abby reflected ruefully that this woman certainly didn't need to worry about competition from her landlady. Her banker's veneer outclassed Abby in every way. Lifting her chin somewhat defensively, Abby said, "Let me just take you over and make sure everything's okay."

Gripping Adam's hand tightly, she walked with fluid strides to the other side of the duplex and unlocked the door. Sloane pressed past her and stood in the doorway, his broad shoulders filling it completely for an instant before giving a decisive nod of approval and stepping inside. He and his wife moved through the empty rooms, their voices echoing hollowly. Abby and Adam stood awkwardly in the living room. Abby tried not to listen in on the conversation, but couldn't help hearing Sloane Jameson's enthusiasm as he checked out his new home.

"This is just perfect, honey!" he called to his wife from the larger of the bedrooms. "It's much better than the apartment. Can you imagine?" he directed at Abby as he came back into the living room, his eyebrow quirked questioningly. "The two of us crammed into a tiny efficiency apartment? It will be great to have some room to spread out."

Abby tried not to be caught staring at him. "I hope you'll be happy here. It's a nice neighborhood," she said politely. She reached deep in the pocket of her denim shorts and pulled out a folded sheet of paper. As she handed it to him, her fingers brushed his and she had the wildest urge to jump back. "This is a list of phone numbers you might find helpful. Mine, of course, if you need anything. The numbers you call to set up your utilities, and the number for all the local papers. And, last but not least, the number for the best pizza in town.

Free delivery!" Abby winked at him broadly.

Sloane turned his smile up a notch. "That is important," he agreed with a full-throated laugh.

"Oh," Abby reached one more time into her pocket and drew out a set of keys, which she dropped, into his outstretched hand, careful not to let her fingers touch his. "Your keys. Please let me know if you need anything." She grabbed Adam's hand and edged toward the door. "I'll see you later. Bye!" She slipped outside and made good her escape into her own side of the duplex.

What on earth had come over her? She'd never acted like that around any man, much less a married one. Especially with his wife standing right next to him. Maybe Ned was right, and she should start dating again. She'd had no shortage of offers, especially from the other pilots she worked with who were drawn to her leggy good looks, long straight hair, and emerald green eyes. Abby maintained an easy friendship with all the guys, but was careful not to get too close to any of them. After her experience with Joe, she wasn't in any hurry to get involved with a man again.

The doorbell rang again. Abby whirled around, half expecting to find Connie Jameson outside, demanding to know what her intentions were toward her husband. But it was only Ned, leaning against the wall of the porch. "Hi, Sis." He aimed a kiss in her direction, but Abby adeptly deflected it with the ease of many long years of practice.

"What is it this time?" she asked.

Ned slouched inside and gave her a look of pure indignation. "They raised my rent," he said. "It's just too much. Not worth it for that dump. So I need a place to hang out till I find new digs."

In other words, thought Abby tiredly, he got evicted for failing to pay the rent again, and plans to try to move in here for as long as he can possibly get away with it. "Well, you can stay here for a few days," she said. "But you know I don't have room for anything longer than that."

"The other side is empty, I noticed." Ned looked at her hopefully.

Abby smiled with satisfaction. "The new tenants are moving in today. Besides, you couldn't possibly afford what I'd charge you for that place."

Ned sighed. "Oh well, guess I'll stow my gear." He started to head back to the bedrooms, but Abby shook her head.

"This is only a two bedroom duplex, Ned," she reminded him. "And both rooms are taken. You'll have to sleep on the couch."

"Why can't I have Adam's room? He has a bed now."

Abby stifled a giggle at the thought of Ned sleeping in Adam's airplane bed. "Adam's too old to sleep with me," she said firmly. "The couch will be fine. Especially since you are only staying a short while."

Ned gave in and deposited his suitcases over in the corner.

"What's for supper?" was his next question.

Abby was sorely tempted to tell him that meals were not included in the deal, but she relented at the puppy-like look in his eyes. Like him or not, he was her stepbrother, and out of deference to the memory of her stepfather, whom she had adored, she would be nice to him. "I thought I'd make spaghetti," she said, knowing it was one of his favorites. "Why don't you play with Adam while I get it on the table?"

Ned nodded eagerly. Whatever his faults, he was a devoted uncle, and Adam worshipped him. Abby left them happily playing with Adam's toy planes on the floor of the living room while she got supper ready. As she walked past the living room window, she caught a glimpse of the Jamesons unloading furniture from a U-haul. Sloane had pulled off his shirt, and she watched, enthralled, as his powerful, well-muscled body moved with easy grace carrying the heavy boxes and furniture. Beads of sweat glistened on his bronzed back, and he exuded masculinity. He effortlessly slung a large carton onto a dolly and straightened up, looking directly at her, his eyes piercing the distance between them. His whole face split into a smile, and she swiveled, quickly turning her back, feeling a warm flush overtake her face.

Abby hurried into the kitchen, wondering how long he'd been aware of her watching him. She knew one thing; she didn't want to meet Sloane Jameson again any time soon. She found his presence much too disturbing.

Sloane surveyed his living room, newly furnished with a casual jumble of bargain basement specials and scrounged up cast-offs. He critically arranged a brass lamp just so on a glass-covered end table by the puffy gray sofa. "What do you think, Con?" he asked.

Connie shuffled wearily into the room and slumped onto the couch. She brushed a strand of curly dark hair out of her eyes and sighed heavily. "What do I think about what? And where's the number she gave us for that pizza?"

Sloane wedged a hand into the pocket of his jeans and pulled out a folded slip of paper. "Maybe our landlady will bring us a casserole like the old days."

"Yeah, you'd like that, I'm sure."

"She is rather pretty," Sloane rubbed his sandpapery chin thoughtfully, giving Connie a rakish grin out of the corner of his eye.

"She could barely keep her eyes off you, you know," Connie said as she hung up the phone after ordering the pizza. "That could be useful to us."

"Perhaps. I don't really fancy it though." Good as he was at his job, he'd never been able to stomach seducing a suspect, even to get essential information. He could never let himself forget that his brother had died because of drugs. That memory was sufficient to kill any attraction he might have felt for any of the people involved in his investigations.

Sloane moved over by the window and looked out. Dusk was falling as the hot Texas sun slipped over the horizon. The street outside was empty, except for someone sitting in a beat-up red car, everybody else evidently inside enjoying their dinners. It appeared to be a nice, quiet neighborhood full of nice, quiet people. Only goes to show you, Sloane thought, curling his lip in disgust, how appearances could be deceiving.

"You okay, Sloane? You're awfully quiet tonight." Connie's words called him back to the present.

Sloane shrugged and let the curtain fall back into place. He didn't feel like explaining how his brief encounter with Abby had left him feeling slightly unsettled inside, had stirred up feelings he didn't want to acknowledge. With a grunt, he changed the subject. "Is the listening gear set up?"

Connie motioned to the bedroom. "Yeah, I thought it would be best to keep it out of sight in case she's the neighborly type."

"I'll go and just listen in, see what they're talking about, if anything. Give me a holler when the pizza gets here."

Connie waved a hand at him. "I'm giving Ron a call."

Sloane made a quick exit to give her privacy for her phone call to her husband. Her real husband that is. Connie made a good partner, but he would never want to be married to her in real life.

He flicked a switch in the box in front of him, and with a crackle the noises in the next duplex became clearly audible. It seemed innocuous enough. Ned was playing with the baby, and Abby was fixing dinner. He could hear her humming an old folk song, could even hear the clank of her spoon against the side of the pan as she beat a soft rhythm to her song. Her voice lulled Sloane into a relaxed mood. They seemed like such ordinary people. Hard to believe they were mixed up in drugs, yet Ned could be arrested right now, should be arrested right now on the strength of the evidence they held at Headquarters. The only reason he was free was the hope that he could lead them to the man in charge.

And Abby... Sloane wrinkled his brow. There was no real evidence against Abby at all. But she was Joe Tarleton's ex-wife. And the letter from Joe had certainly implicated her. Somewhere out there had to be the evidence that would tie her to the ring. He and Connie just had to find it.

He had a hard time thinking of Abby as a drug dealer, though. Instead he kept remembering the sea-green sparkle of her eyes, the electric warmth of her touch. He snorted derisively. He needed a vacation after this assignment. Attracted to Joe Tarleton's wife after just the briefest of encounters? He'd been working much too hard lately.

The shrill sound of the telephone cut through the peaceful, domestic setting. "Hello?" Abby said in her slightly breathy voice. Sloane pressed a button on his equipment that enabled him to listen to both sides of the conversation.

"Yeah. This is Micky. I need to double my usual. Same place. Bye." The voice on the other end growled the words so quickly that Sloane could barely understand him. Fortunately the listening equipment was set up so that all conversations were automatically recorded on tape.

"Wait a minute!" Abby's voice, high and slightly impatient, came over the line, but it was too late. The caller had hung up.

Sloane made a temple with his hands, his eyebrows creased with surprise. With a flick of a switch he replayed the conversation, nodding with satisfaction as the words unfolded. He'd not even been on the job twenty-four hours and already had the first concrete bit of evidence tying Abby Tarleton to the drug ring.

He heard the clink of plates on the table, and then Abby called Ned and Adam in to eat. Sloane closed his eyes and listened. Abby's throaty voice sent a thrill through him, and he again reminded himself that not only was she Joe Tarleton's wife but she was probably a drug runner in her own right. As such he could not be attracted to her.

CHAPTER TWO

"So, what do you hear from Joe?" Ned asked as he stuffed the last half of a breadstick into his mouth, scattering crumbs all over his shirt.

Abby, the strange phone call she had received completely forgotten, evenly poured spaghetti sauce over her pasta and twirled the noodles on her fork. "Nothing," she said flatly, casting an eye at Adam.

"Nothing?"

"Nothing," Abby said with quiet emphasis.

"He ought to be getting out soon," Ned continued.

Abby shrugged. "Makes no difference to me." Her voice was cold and distant.

"Come on, Abs. He made a mistake."

Abby's voice hardened as she retorted tartly. "Yeah, he was stupid. And so was I."

Ned hastily swallowed the last of his spaghetti. "Great supper, Sis. I've got to go out. Can you give me a key? It'd save me having to wake you up when I come in."

Abby frowned but dug an extra key out of one of the drawers. "All right, but try to be quiet coming in. I have an early flight."

She flinched as Ned banged the front door. He seemed absolutely unable to go anywhere without making noise. She glanced at her watch and idly wondered what the new neighbors were doing. Maybe she should go over and check; she normally did when tenants moved in. But she really didn't want to encounter Sloane Jameson again. She found being near him just too unnerving.

Connie looked at Sloane as she grabbed the last slice of pizza, which had come just as Abby and Ned had started eating their dinner. Together she and Sloane had been eating and listening in silence to the conversation next door.

"You know," said Connie, as she swallowed. "Now would be a good time for me to go shopping and for you to get locked out of the house."

Sloane nodded thoughtfully. It made sense to try to develop a rapport with Abby as soon as possible. It was the way he and Connie worked--he usually gained the suspect's confidence while Connie followed the paper trail and tracked down leads. Her prickly personality made it hard for them to switch roles, yet this time he wished they could. Abby Tarleton made him uneasy for some reason.

Something about her made it difficult for him to remember her connection with the drug ring; that people were having their lives ruined every day by people like Ned, Joe, and probably Abby; that his own brother had been killed by drugs. However, he had a job to do, and he was not going to let Abby Tarleton stop him, no matter how bewitching her smile or how tantalizing her eyes. He waited for Connie to leave and then stood up, taking one final gulp of his cola. Time to go to work.

Abby made a clicking sound with her tongue as she wiped spaghetti off of Adam's face, hands, ears, neck, and even his shoes. He loved spaghetti but oh, what a mess he made! Actually, spaghetti was one of the few things she cooked well, but as she always said, it didn't take much talent to throw a few cans together and shake in some spices. As she started to clear the table, the doorbell rang. She opened the door and took a quick, sharp breath when she saw Sloane Jameson leaning casually against the outside wall. She could feel the heat emanating from his body, and she felt distinctly weak at the knees at the sight of the wisps of dark hair curled against the v-neck of his shirt.

"Oh, hello," she stammered, hoping she didn't sound as startled as she felt. Her slender hands unconsciously twisted together.

"Hi." His tone was apologetic. "I'm sorry to bother you, but I seem to have locked myself out of the house. Do you have an extra key? I'll bring it right back." His eyes moved slowly over her body, taking in her smooth bosom and her long, lithe thighs.

Abby was very much aware of his appraisal. A blush crept like a shadow over her cheeks, and she quickly turned away, letting her hair drape across her face to hide her discomfort. "I'll let you in," she said.

"I hate to put you to the trouble," Sloane said quickly, giving her a smile that sent her pulse racing. "I could take the key and bring it right back."

"No problem," Abby said firmly. "I meant to come over anyway and see how you were doing. Just let me grab my little boy. Adam!" she called. "Let's go for a walk."

The three-year-old willingly left his airplanes and thrust his sturdy hand into hers. Mother and child made a charming picture, and Sloane wondered that such a seemingly nice person could be caught up in the sordid world of drugs. With a grand sweep of his hand, he stood aside, allowing them to pass through the door. Jingling the keys in the pocket of her shorts, Abby walked next door,

Sloane falling easily into step beside her.

Abby bent forward and fit her key into the lock, conscious of Sloane's eyes watching her every move. "Here," she said, giving it a deft twist. "That should do it." She straightened her shoulders and transferred her gaze to him.

For a moment his gaze held hers as he studied her intently. His eyes swept down her body, and she shivered, even in the heat of the summer evening. She licked her lips and folded her arms protectively across her chest as a slow flush started in her cheeks. Sloane noted her discomfort and broke into a leisurely smile in an attempt to put her at ease. "Thanks a lot. I'm awfully sorry to have disturbed you," he said ruefully.

"No problem. That's why I'm here. Are you getting settled in okay?" she asked in her low, dusty voice, her eyes lingering on the dark hair curling across his forehead.

In answer, Sloane motioned her inside with a sweeping motion of his hand. His fingers brushed against the bared curve of her shoulders, sending a warm tingle down her spine. "Pretty much. We don't have a lot of our stuff yet. But I think we'll be happy here."

Abby took in the spartan nature of the furnishings, and her mouth curved into an unconscious smile at the sight of the worn, old couch. "That looks comfortable," she said.

"Yeah, Connie hates it. But I've had it since I left home and just can't bring myself to part with it." His stance emphasized the force of his thighs and the slimness of his hips.

Abby realized she was staring again and quickly shifted her gaze to the pizza carton on the coffee table. "Did you enjoy it?" she asked lightly.

"Delicious. You were right, it is pretty good." Sloane looked briefly over her shoulder out the window. "Is that your husband that just pulled up?"

Abby stiffened, and the color drained from her face. She turned around to look outside and then relaxed. "No, that's my brother, Ned. He's staying with me for a while." Her smile thinned as she spoke.

Sloane pressed closer behind her, so close she could feel his warm breath tickling the hair on the back of her neck. Abby turned to look at him, amazed at the thrill she felt at being so close to him. He stared back at her, seemingly unaware of the effect he was having upon her. "Bet your husband likes that." Despite an odd reluctance to do so, Sloane pressed hard, needing to see her reaction to the mention of her husband.

He was disappointed however. Abby jauntily tossed her hair over her shoulder and shook her head. "I'm divorced," she said as casually as she could manage.

"I'm sorry," Sloane said, wondering if he dared push any harder. He didn't want to arouse Abby's suspicions, he told himself, deciding to back off.

"I'm not." Abby adroitly ducked behind him and turned to examine a row of framed photos, mostly landscapes, leaning against the wall, waiting to be hung up. She cocked an eyebrow. "Are these yours?"

"Yeah." Sloane held his breath as she examined his work. He needn't have worried. Abby gracefully knelt down to give the photos a closer look, then she raised her face to his, her emerald eyes sparkling with pleasure.

"They're wonderful! I remember now. Your wife said you were a photojournalist."

"Freelance." Not for the first time Sloane reflected that his journalism degree came in handy in his undercover work. He was a lousy writer, he knew, but as a photographer, he wasn't half bad.

Abby shook her head admiringly. "I'm very impressed. You have quite a talent."

"Thanks." Her unrestrained praise made him feel self-conscious, and Sloane looked wildly around for a moment, grasping for something to change the subject to. Adam ran around the room, making airplane noises. Sloane crouched down in his path, and the little boy reluctantly slid to a stop. "What's your name?" Sloane asked.

"Adam."

"You like airplanes, Adam?" Sloane's voice was surprisingly gentle. Abby admired his easy manner with her son.

"Yeah! When I grow up, I'm gonna be a pilot like my mommy."

Sloane stood up and turned back to Abby, pushing his hands deep into his pockets. "You're a pilot? That's interesting. I don't know many women pilots. Do you fly for an airline?"

"I fly freight out of the Robinville Airport, on the edge of town," Abby said, still examining the photos. "Strictly small planes. The jets aren't any fun to fly. It's all computerized now. I like to feel I'm really in control."

Sloane leaned back, sizing her up. "Maybe someday I could do a story on you."

Abby shook her head and smiled smoothly. "I'm really not a very interesting person." She glanced at her watch. "I'd better go now. I have an early flight tomorrow. Let me know if I can be of any further help." With a deliberately casual movement she took Adam's hand and left the duplex.

Sloane stared after her, a frown creasing his brow. He was intrigued by the smooth manner in which she gave out only as much information about herself as she wanted known and no more. Most suspects that he had investigated had been more furtive and wary. Only a few of the really good ones had developed the same easygoing way that Abby had of discouraging questions.

He watched as she and Adam walked leisurely to their own door. Abby paused halfway across the yard and looked across the street at the old red car Sloane had noticed earlier. Her stance stiffened almost imperceptibly, and then she shook her head ever so slightly and continued on her way to the door. Adam tugged at her hand and stopped to point out a grasshopper. Abby tenderly scooped the bug into her cupped hand so Adam could examine it closely.

Sloane suppressed a smile at the sight of the two golden heads bent over the insect. Abby's finger delicately pointed out parts of the grasshopper body, while Adam's brow furrowed in concentration as he listened to his mother's soft voice. After a few moments, the lesson over, Abby set the grasshopper on a blade of grass and challenged Adam in a hopping contest to the door. They collapsed, laughing, on the steps. Then Abby grabbed her son and tucked him inside the house.

Sloane remained in a thoughtful silence by the window for a moment. He cast an eye at the red car that had spooked Abby. A newspaper obscured the driver's face. Sloane automatically glanced at the license plate, noting that it was covered with mud. With a mental shrug, he went into the bedroom to check the listening equipment. A flashing light told him that someone had used the phone next door. He ran the tape and listened as Ned's voice spoke in a frantic tone to a voice at the other end.

"Yeah, I'm at Abby's for a while. Don't know how long I can stay here though."

"They can find you there easy enough," the voice said.

"Yeah, I know. But they wouldn't dare bother me here I don't think."

"You're probably right. The heat's really on though. You'd better just lie low for a while."

"I won't stick my nose out. Gotta go now." With a click the conversation ended.

Sloane leaned back in his chair, rubbing his chin thoughtfully. So Ned was hiding out. But from whom? Did he think the police were on to him? Or was he hiding from someone in the gang? And if it was the gang, why wouldn't they dare to bother him while he was at Abby's? Could she possibly hold more power in the gang than they had suspected? It was hard to believe. She seemed so nice. But Sloane knew from experience that some of the nicest people you could ever hope to meet were drug dealers.

Abby heard a car door slam. Glancing out the window, she saw Connie hurrying up the steps next door, two grocery bags in her arms.

Guiltily, Abby slipped away from the window into the kitchen, afraid Connie would look straight through the walls of her house and see the lustful thoughts going through Abby's mind about her husband. Hard as she tried, she could not put Sloane from her mind. She searched through a haze of feelings and desires, trying to make sense of her jumbled emotions. Why did this man affect her so deeply? She couldn't deny the physical attraction she felt for him, but there was more to it than that. He had been so gentle with Adam; he genuinely seemed to like kids, and his admiration for her flying career had seemed sincere.

Most of the men she encountered were male chauvinists with little regard for small children--"Why don't you run along, sonny, and let me talk to your mother?"--or for women pilots--"A purty little thing like you flying one of them great big planes? Imagine that!"

Abby shook her head and nibbled on her lip. Sloane's face haunted her, a phantom that refused to leave her mind. Her face burned as she remembered the unnerving sensation that had swept through her body when his hand had brushed ever so softly against her shoulder.

She just couldn't make sense of it. What had happened to the levelheaded young woman of yesterday? Then she had been a calm, cool, collected person with no interest in men at all. Today she had been transformed into a brazen young hussy who had all but thrown herself at a married man!

Abby drew a deep breath and imposed an iron control on herself. What she was feeling was nothing more than a silly, physical infatuation, and she would just have to make an extra effort to keep her relationship with Sloane on a strictly business-like level. The last thing she needed was to get involved with a married man.

She was roused from her reverie when Ned clomped into the room. "Okay, Sis. I got Adam to bed snug as a bug in a rug. Got any beer?" Her stepbrother opened the refrigerator door and rummaged inside.

"No." Abby's nose wrinkled in distaste. "Ned, how long are you going to be here?"

"Not long. Just till I find another place," Ned said evasively.

"How long will that take? A day?" Abby faced him squarely with both hands on her hips.

"Sis!"

"Two days?" Abby persisted, her lips puckered with annoyance.

"Don't you want me here?" Ned asked plaintively.

"Not really. The last time you were here all your friends started showing up and expecting me to feed them at all hours of the night. I won't have people like that around Adam." Abby's voice was smooth but insistent.

"Aw, come on, Sis. They're harmless."

"Maybe. But their language is filthy and they treat me like dirt. This is my house, and I won't stand for it." Her voice raised slightly.

"All right, Sis. I promise. No guests."

Abby gritted her teeth. "How long, Ned?"

"Give me a week," Ned pleaded. "Time to find another apartment."

Abby sighed. "All right, Ned. One week. Then you're out of here."

"Of course, Sis. Whatever you say."

Sloane and Connie looked at each other. Connie raised her eyebrows. "Well, it appears Momma doesn't want the baby involved in the family business."

Sloane shook his head. "Maybe Momma has bigger plans for the baby. I'm thinking Abby Tarleton may be higher up in the scheme of things than we ever dreamed. According to Neddie boy, the gang doesn't dare bother him when he's at her house."

"Oh really?" Connie nodded thoughtfully. "I wonder why not?"

"Could be they don't want to get into trouble with Abby. We've been thinking her job flying freight is just a cover for drug running.

But what if when she's flying freight, she's really visiting the dealers?"

"Could be. That would fit."

Sloane sighed with satisfaction. "I think we'd better keep a very close watch on Abby Tarleton. This could be more important than we suspected."

CHAPTER THREE

Abby unfastened the straps of Adam's car seat and lifted him out of the car. With a pat on the bottom, she sent him running toward the house. Bending her elbows and placing her hands on the small of her back, she stretched, cat-like. She swept her gaze across the street and saw, with a churning mixture of dismay, fear, and anger that sank to the pit of her stomach like a rock that the all too familiar red Chevy was parked across the street once more.

A sudden burst of rage surged through her and without thinking, Abby marched across the street, head held high and eyes flashing, to confront the driver. He looked up from his newspaper, a startled expression on his face, as Abby leaned in the open window. She noted and tucked away in the back of her mind details of the man's appearance, a tanned face that would be considered ruggedly good looking were it not marred by a bulbous, large pored nose. Abby was not surprised to see three empty beer cans littering the floor of the car.

"Can I help you?" she asked in a voice heavy with

sarcasm. Her annoyance increased when she noticed her hands shaking. She clenched them tightly to her sides in an effort to control the tremors.

The man was nonplused by her words. He just stared back at her, left eyebrow raised in a supercilious sneer.

Abby took a deep breath and continued. "You've been sitting in this eyesore of a car outside my house off and on for the past three weeks. You've even followed me around town. Now, before I call the police, I just want to know why. Are you one of Ned's friends?"

The man smiled at her with smoke-stained teeth. "No, lady," he said in a voice that was surprisingly high for a man's. "I wouldn't call myself a friend of Ned's. And if you are smart, you'll forget all about me and try not to notice things so much next time."

He suddenly reached down and held up a brown, paper-wrapped package that he thrust into her hands. Abby held onto the package by sheer reflex, and stood rooted to the spot, blank, amazed, and very shaken as the man started his car and with a nonchalant wave of his hand squealed off.

Abby's eyes followed him till he disappeared around the corner. Then she forced her leaden feet to move toward the duplex, still clutching the package in her hands, absent-mindedly tearing the paper open. She exhaled sharply as she saw sheaths of green peeking through the brown paper. Looking more closely she found three thick bundles of fifty-dollar bills.

"Oh Ned!" she thought, holding the package to her chest. "What have you done now?"

On the other side of the duplex, Sloane dropped the sheet, white curtain, shielding himself from her sight. What a brazen move on her part, he thought. He had recognized the man as soon as he had lowered his newspaper. He was a well-known drug dealer who usually stuck to the shadier side of town. It was unusual for him to venture out into the better neighborhoods.

Sloane slapped his fist into his palm in frustration. If only he'd had time to record the transaction between Abby and the dealer on film, but it had happened much too quickly. Before he had realized what was happening, it was over.

Perhaps that was why she did it like that, mused Sloane. To keep people off guard. Still, the boldness of the move bothered him.

Especially from such a cagey operator as Abby obviously was. Sloane realized that he was even more bothered by the look on her face as she had opened the package of money--shocked disbelief, fear, and anger. A strange reaction to have to a routine payment drop.

Sloane shrugged dismissively. The important thing was that he had witnessed a large amount of money changing hands between Abby and a known drug dealer. The rest would become clear once he and Connie finished exposing Abby's sordid game.

Abby slammed the door as she stepped inside her home. She desperately wanted to have it out with Ned. She was convinced that he had something to do with the man watching her house and the big bundle of money she had just received, but she didn't dare bring it up with Adam around. However, when she saw the state her living room was in, her anger boiled over, and when Ned raised his hand in a friendly wave, her pent-up fury exploded. "Look at this mess!" Her eyes flashed at her stepbrother. "Ned, what have you been doing all day? I don't need to come home to this!"

"Sorry, Sis," Ned said contritely, scrambling up from the sofa where he had been sitting drinking a beer and watching TV. The floor was littered with empty cans, half open sheets of newspaper, and the remains of Ned's breakfast and lunch, not to mention his dirty socks and underwear. "I'm just not used to picking up after myself."

"Well, you'd better get used to it," Abby picked up a beer can and chunked it into a nearby trashcan. "I won't stand for this, Ned."

"I'll clean it up, Sis. I promise. You don't have a thing to worry about," Ned swooped down and began grabbing the newspapers off the floor. He caught a glimpse of his nephew out of the corner of his eye and swung around. "Hey, Adam, my man! How's tricks?"

"Boy, Uncle Ned, you sure drink a lot of beer." Adam stood in the center of the room and looked around, eyes wide with wonder, index finger slightly extended as he started to count the cans.

"Ned-" Abby began warningly.

"Yeah, right little Tiger. Let me get this cleaned up real quick for your mom. Come on Abs. I can see you're tired. Let me take you and Adam to McDonald's® for supper."

"All right!" Adam jumped up and down and made airplane noises to express his excitement.

"I'm really too tired to go out, Ned," Abby protested.

"No, you're not. It's either that or you fix supper for us, and I know you're too tired to do that. Come on, Sis. I'm buying."

"All right," Abby conceded. "But get this mess cleaned up first."

"Oh, I will, I will. You go freshen up and I'll have it looking ship shape by the time you're done."

Sloane sat back and made a temple with his hands, replaying the conversation in his head. Nothing incriminating to either one of them there. Just a normal, domestic conversation. But hadn't Abby been furious though! He wondered at the relationship between them.

Ned seemed to be almost scared of his sister, although he would have bet money that Ned was also deliberately trying to make his sister angry. Was the conflict between them a reflection of their criminal activities or did it go farther back to their family life? Ned was only Abby's stepbrother. Maybe they'd never gotten along. Oh well, Sloane thought. He was not likely to find the answer to that problem any time soon. He wasn't even sure why he cared. It was nothing to him if his suspect didn't get along with her stepbrother. He needed to focus on the job at hand. He'd been waiting all day for the other side of the duplex to be empty. Now was his chance. While they were both gone, he would take the opportunity to search their side of the duplex.

He waited till he heard Abby, Ned, and Adam leaving to go out to eat. Grabbing his lock pit kit, Sloane didn't waste a minute. "Keep watch, Connie," he called as he went out the door. He knew she would station herself by the window and let him know as soon as she saw Ned's car return. They had worked together for so long that they could almost communicate without words.

Abby stuck her last french fry in her mouth and watched as Adam climbed up the slide at the playground at McDonald's. She and Ned were seated at an outside table so Adam could play after he ate. They were the only ones outside, which gave them a modicum of privacy. Abby took a deep, shaky breath. What she had to say to Ned just couldn't wait any longer. She had to find out now, while no one else was around to hear, exactly what he was involved in. Drawing her purse to her, she opened it and showed him the bundles of money. "What do you know about this, Ned?" she asked in an ominous tone.

Ned's eyes widened as they traveled from Abby's cold, disapproving face to the piles of money filling her purse. "Me!" he squeaked. "Nothing! Wish I did, though. Where'd you get it, Sis?"

Eagerly he reached out and rifled through the bills, counting them under his breath.

Abby snatched the bundles away from him and tucked them safely into her purse, nervously aware of her surroundings. She took a quick look around to make sure she and Ned were still alone and then spoke in a low voice. "From a man who's been watching the house, and me, for about three weeks." Briefly Abby told Ned about her confrontation with the man. When she was finished she asked tersely, "Now I want you to tell me what you have to do with this, Ned. What sort of trouble are you in?"

Ned looked at her with innocent eyes. "This has nothing to do with me, Sis. I'll admit to having a disagreement with some of my friends, but from what you say, this guy started watching you long before that. Besides, giving money away is not their usual way of settling an argument."

"Then you don't mind if I turn this money over to the police?" Abby asked in a calculating tone, fully expecting him to protest.

"It would be more fun to spend it." Ned cast a hopeful look at her purse.

"Ned!" Abby's voice held a warning that even he couldn't ignore.

"All right. All right. No. Go ahead and turn it in. The money's not mine."

Abby pierced him with her fiercest glare. As far as she could see, he was telling the truth. And he had never been able to lie to her. With a troubled sigh she decided to believe him. She was relieved that he was not involved with the money, but the question was still left open of to whom the money belonged and why it had been given to her.

The first thing Sloane did upon entering the home next door was unlock the back door so he could make a quick get away, if necessary. Then he looked around the living room. Nothing met his eye, but he knew that any evidence would be pretty well hidden. He did a hurried search of Ned's bag, finding, as he had suspected, a tiny bag of white powder at the bottom. He left it untouched, and continued his search. Tucked into one of Ned's socks, he found a letter and pulled it out to read. It was from Joe, letting Ned know the good news, that he had received an early release from prison because of overcrowding. Sloane's eyebrows knitted together in a scowl. Although he had already known about this, indeed, it was the reason for his current assignment; he didn't have to like it. Scum like Joe Tarleton should never be allowed back on the streets.

The next part of the note was more interesting. Joe planned to visit Ned at Abby's house. Sloane grunted at the date. It was two days away. He folded the letter and put it back into the envelope, tapping it thoughtfully against his palm. A tight smile crossed his face. That meeting promised to be very interesting. He would have to make a point of being at his listening post then.

Sloane put the letter back into the socks and tucked them carefully away in the bag. Then he moved around the living room, searching carefully for more evidence. He ran his hands around the picture frames on the wall and paused to look admiringly at the photos of the Navy Blue Angels flying in formation. He ruffled through the books on the shelf, mostly paperback novels and children's books. He took a little more time with Abby's desk, but found only neat stacks of bills, the checks already written and ready for mailing, and careful records of her finances for the past several months. Sloane scrutinized these closely but found nothing untoward in them. If she was receiving any money from illegal means, she kept it separate from her personal finances.

Next Sloane went into her bedroom and paused to absorb the different atmosphere. A soft scent lingered and the room was surprisingly feminine. A double bed stood invitingly in the corner with a white, eyelet lace coverlet arranged carefully over a rose-colored satin sheet. A white wicker dressing table was crowded with bottles and jars. Sloane cast a practiced eye over them but found only cosmetics and perfumes. A wicker nightstand held a princess telephone, with a photo of Abby and Adam standing by an airplane.

He picked the picture up to examine it more closely.

It was evidently fairly recent; Adam didn't look much younger than he was now. The little boy stood on a block in front of the plane while Abby stood beside him with her arm around him. They were both wearing blue coveralls, and Abby's hair was pulled back into a ponytail. Both their faces were split into wide grins, and it was easy to see that they were where they most loved to be. A muscle quivered at Sloane's jaw, and he quickly set the picture back on the table and moved on to Abby's chest of drawers.

He opened the top drawer and drew his breath in sharply. Neat piles of frilly lingerie met his eyes. He ran his hands lingeringly over the lacy lingerie and silky gowns with a faint sense of surprise. He had thought Abby would probably sleep in an old t-shirt with socks and cotton underwear, but a smile etched his lips as he thought of her wearing one of the flowing gowns in his hands. He rubbed the gown between his fingers, relishing its cool, slippery feel against his skin. A different image of her flitted through his mind, a soft, winsome Abby, and for a moment he stood lost in his daydream. If he closed his eyes, he could see her, her body perfectly outlined by the lamp behind her, its tantalizing secrets barely hidden by the filmy white material of the gown. She moved toward him, the gown billowing around her as she floated over the floor, a gentle smile lighting her face. A smile just for him. He could almost feel the warmth of her skin beneath the material, could almost hear her sigh of pleasure as he bent to kiss her.

His dead brother's face supplanted hers and Sloane's fantasy shattered abruptly. How could he even think of kissing her? Even if she were not involved with the drug ring herself, she had been Joe Tarleton's wife. A tiny voice in the back of his mind said insistently that she was an attractive woman, but Sloane pushed that thought away. No one involved with drugs was attractive. Sloane dropped Abby's gown as though it were a beehive and moved to search Abby's closet.

There her clothes were more sensible. Jeans and sweaters. Sweatshirts and polo shirts. A few skirts and blouses. Some jumpers. One nice dress. A quick search of the shelves turned up nothing of interest. Sloane moved on and finally, tucked away behind a box of photo albums, he found a tiny stack of letters. Rifling through them, he found they were all from Joe. Most of them had been written from prison. Sloane ignored these as they already had copies of them provided by the prison censors. He pulled the earlier letters out, but before he could look through them, the phone shrilled half a ring and he hurriedly stuffed the letters back on the shelf.

That short ring was Connie's signal that Abby was back. Still clutching the one letter he'd started to read,

Sloane made a dash for the back door. By the time Abby, Adam, and Ned opened the front door of their home, he was sitting innocently on the sofa in his living room.

"Find anything?" Connie asked.

"Yes and no. Abby must be too smart to keep anything at the house. But Ned apparently doesn't have as much on the ball as his sister. Found some coke and a letter from Joe setting up a meeting at Abby's place the day after tomorrow."

Connie whistled. “Is that it in your hand?"

Sloane looked down, puzzled for a moment. Then his blue eyes cleared. "Oh, she's keeping a stack of letters from her hubby in her closet. I pulled an old one out to read and forgot I had it." Unfolding the letter, Sloane scanned the lines.

"Anything?"

Sloane shook his head and handed her the letter. "Just mushy stuff about everlasting love and all that. Joe seems to be a real romantic guy," he said lightly. Inside, he was more disturbed by the letter than he let on. Unaccountably he hated to think of Abby receiving passionate love letters from Joe.

Connie nodded disinterestedly. "Did that letter to Ned mention Abby?"

"No, he just said he'd meet Ned at Abby's."

"That should be an interesting meeting." Connie puffed her cheeks out. "How about tonight I investigate the hangar and plane while you keep an eye on our friends?"

Sloane nodded. "Sounds good to me."

Connie left the room to get ready for her night activities while Sloane settled in the listening room to read over the latest reports on Abby's airfreight company. It was hard to concentrate; despite his efforts to banish it, Abby's face lingered on the edges of his mind. Finally he leaned back and closed his eyes. As he did, Abby's voice crackled over the speaker. "Ned, what were you doing in my room?"

Sloane sat bolt upright. He looked furtively around, hoping Connie was not within earshot, but she stood in the doorway, having come in when she'd heard the voices. She raised a delicately arched eyebrow at him. Sloane put his hand over his face and sat back to listen.

"I haven't been in your room, Abs. I swear!" Ned's voice sounded hurt.

"Don't give me that!" Abby said sharply. "My drawers are all messed up. We're not kids anymore, Ned. You're getting a little old to go through my underwear."

Sloane peered at Connie through his fingers. She had her hand over her mouth in a futile attempt not to laugh.

"It wasn't me, Sis. I swear!" Ned's voice took on a rising note of desperation.

"Were you looking for money or what?" Abby's fury was relentless. "Well now you know that there isn't any. So keep out from now on!" There was a dead silence and then the quiet sound of a door closing, its softness ever so much more effective than a slam would have been.

Sloane slid down in his chair, afraid to look at Connie, who was doubled over with laughter. "Lucky for you she had Ned to blame!" Connie gasped when she could speak again. "Tell me, Sloane, where exactly did you learn your search technique?"

"I was just being thorough," Sloane said stiffly, trying to maintain his dignity.

Still laughing, Connie left the room to finish getting ready for her evening search of Abby's hangar. Once she was gone, Sloane relaxed, a faint smile tracing his lips as he thought of the filmy, silken gowns he'd found in Abby's room. A warm glow suffused his entire body as he remembered the feel of the gown slipping between his fingers. What would Abby look like draped in that gown, he wondered. He felt a stab of desire at the thought and shivered slightly. He couldn't remember ever feeling this way about a suspect before. Resolutely he sat up and turned once more to his reports, but it was hopeless. He simply could not get his vision of a white-gowned Abby Tarleton out of his mind.

CHAPTER FOUR

Abby discontentedly threw her book down on the bed beside herself. Her head throbbed angrily, and she opened the drawer of her wicker nightstand, reaching for the bottle of aspirin she kept inside. Between the stress of Ned parking himself in her living room, the strange man who had been following her, and the disturbing feelings she felt for Sloane Jameson, she felt as though she were in a trap with a noose slowly tightening around her neck. The phone beside the bed jangled, and she hurriedly took a gulp of water to push the aspirin down and picked up the receiver. "Hello?" she said in a taut voice.

"It's Rex. Cut my order by half. Too much heat."

There was a soft click, and Abby was left staring at the phone. She shook her head, brushed her hair out of her eyes, and thought to herself that someone certainly had the wrong number. She put the phone down and padded into the bathroom. Maybe a nice, hot shower would help soothe her frayed nerves.

Sloane nodded with satisfaction as he listened once more to the tape of the phone call. The evidence was mounting up quite nicely. With any luck, Connie's search of Abby's office at the airport would be successful, and they would be well on their way to wrapping up the case. He felt a grudging admiration for Abby. She was very canny, always careful not to say anything that might incriminate herself, but he knew they'd get her in the end. They always did.

He heard the rush of water from her shower. Her soft voice rose above the water, singing an old folk song he remembered from when he was a child. "Oh, ye'll take the high road, and I'll take the low road." The notes floated liltingly around his head, and he listened with genuine enjoyment. She had a lovely singing voice with clear, smooth tones.

"For me and my true love will never meet again," Abby continued.

Sloane wondered if she had a true love, if Joe had been her true love. He closed his eyes and felt a familiar stirring within him as he imagined what she must look like right at that moment, totally bare with water splattering over her body. It was a pleasant thought and for a moment he forgot completely about his assignment, forgot completely that Abby was his quarry until the noise of the shower stopped, and his fantasy came to an abrupt end.

Abby stepped out of the shower and groped blindly for a towel. She felt much better; the pulsing spray of water had soothed and relaxed her poor, strained muscles. As she rubbed her hair dry, she heard the phone ring again. She hesitated, hoping Ned would answer it, but she should have known better. He had probably fallen asleep in front of the TV again. The phone rang a second time and with a muffled exclamation, she wrapped a towel around herself and ran into the bedroom.

She paused with her hand hovering over the receiver, strangely reluctant to answer it. What if it was another of those strange calls, she wondered. With the fifth ring she caved in and snatched the phone out of its cradle. "Hello?"

"Hello, Abby?"

Abby heaved a sigh of relief as she recognized Jerry, a pilot she knew from the airport. She sat on the edge of the bed. "Yes, Jerry, what do you want?"

"You letting someone work in your office?" he asked.

Abby raised her eyebrows and continued toweling

her hair. "No. Why? Is someone there?"

"Well, I really don't know for sure. Saw some lights in there just after I got back from doing some night flying."

Trying to impress a new girlfriend with the lights of Fort Worth and Dallas from above thought Abby to herself with a knowing smile.

"Looked kind of like a flashlight," Jerry continued.

"I see," said Abby slowly as she tried to think of what to do. Normally she would charge over to the airport, but these past few days had really spooked her. Ail of the odd happenings made her think twice before rushing headlong into danger.

"Um, Abby? Is there anything you need me to do? It's not the most convenient time, but if you need help, just ask."

Abby heard the sound of a female voice in the background and rolled her eyes. Jerry never could keep a girlfriend. He was a bit of a jerk. A nice jerk, but still a jerk. "No, Jerry. Go ahead. I'll take it from here. Thanks a lot."

Sloane drummed his fingers on the table in front of him with a rising sense of alarm. Abby's friend must have spotted Connie's flashlight." Quickly he dialed Connie's cell phone and listened to it ring without answer. It went to voice mail and Sloane left a quick message of warning. He knew as he hung up that there was no guarantee that Connie would get the message. She probably had her cell phone on silent mode and, knowing her, she probably hadn't set it on vibrate.

Abby's voice came over the speaker in a low, determined manner. "I'd better get out there," she said in a voice clearly meant only for herself.

Sloane sprang into action. Somehow he had to stop Abby from going to the airport, or make sure she took him along for the ride.

Abby let the towel fall to the floor at her feet and reached blindly into her closet, throwing on the first clothes that came to hand, old cut-off denim shorts, a white pullover shirt, and sneakers but no socks. As she walked through the living room, her upper lip curled in distaste at the sight of Ned sprawled on the couch, eyes closed, mouth agape, his filthy shoes propped on the cream-colored armrest. She briefly wondered if she should wake him and tell him where she was going, but decided against it. She would probably be back before he ever knew she was gone. Just in case she left a note taped to the television. For the first time she was grateful for his presence; at least she didn't need to worry about leaving Adam alone.

Abby slipped softly out the front door and was brought up short by the sight of Sloane lounging casually on his front porch. "Hi." He waved at her in a friendly manner.

"Hi," Abby said, and without giving him a second glance, hurried to her car. As she wrestled with the lock, she heard soft footsteps and knew without turning around that Sloane had come up behind her.

"You seem to be in a hurry," he said, his voice reverberating comfortingly in her ear. "Is something wrong?"

Abby wavered, torn between her natural inclination to handle things on her own, and her reluctance to investigate the intruder by herself. She caught Sloane's eyes looking at her with concern and made a quick decision to confide in him. "I've got to go out to the airport. A friend of mine saw some lights in my office at the hangar, and I need to check it out." The words tumbled out of her mouth, and Abby realized her heart was thudding in her chest. She took a deep breath to calm herself down.

Sloane nodded thoughtfully. "Have you called the police?" There was an odd tone to his voice.

"No." Abby shook her head decisively. "I want to check it out for myself first. It may not be anything."

"What about airport security? Shouldn't they

investigate things like this?" Sloane continued.

Abby wished he would stop questioning her and let her get on with her business. She yanked open the door of her car, ready to slide inside. "Security?" she said impatiently. "One old man who's probably sleeping off a bender. I've got to check it out myself."

Sloane rounded the other side of the car. "I can't let you go by yourself. I'll come along."

Surprise swept across Abby's face. "It might be dangerous," she protested.

"All the more reason for me to come along. Now open the door." Sloane's voice had an imperious note that Abby didn't dare ignore.

She unlocked the passenger door and started the engine. She had the car in motion before Sloane the door closed. "Thanks for coming with me, Sloane," she said, suddenly feeling unaccountably shy.

"No problem," said Sloane. Especially since it gave him a chance to make sure Connie was in the clear, he thought. Had his partner been careless, or just a victim of bad luck, he wondered. Either way, he was going to personally change the settings on her cell phone the next time he saw her.

Either way, he hoped she was out of the office by the time they got there. If not, well, he would have to play it by ear. Somehow he had to get into the hangar before Abby and give Connie a chance to escape.

The short ride to the airport was made in silence, both lost in their thoughts. Abby was focused on the latest incidence of unreality. Was someone really going through her office, or had Jerry merely imagined it? She kept no money at the hangar, nothing of any importance to anyone else. She could not come up with a single reason why anyone would go through her office, but then she couldn't figure out why anyone would follow her, either, or give her a pack of money and drive away. Her mind spun with bewilderment. Nothing seemed to make sense anymore. She shook her head in puzzled frustration and glanced at Sloane sitting next to her. His head was turned slightly as he stared out the window, apparently lost in thoughts of his own. To her surprise, she was glad he had come along. He exuded an air of confident security that calmed her fears.

Almost before she knew it, Abby reached the gates of the airport. She swung her car into a parking space well away from her hangar. Noting Sloane's look of surprise, she explained, "If there is an intruder, I don't want to take a chance of having him see us."

Sloane nodded approvingly. "That's sensible. Why don't you wait here, while I check things out? If I'm not back in fifteen minutes, you can call the police."

Abby's lips trembled with the need to smile. She patted Sloane on the cheek. "Cute, Sloane, cute. Now let's get real."

Sloane shrugged sheepishly. Oh well. He had known it wasn't likely to work, but he'd had to try.

"Now," continued Abby, her voice brisk and business-like again. "My office is on the other side of this hangar. If we just hug the wall, we should make it there without disturbing whoever's inside, if anybody."

Sloane nodded. "Sounds like a plan to me. Let's go." They crept along the wall of the hangar, inching agonizingly past the corrugated metal, their hands feeling their way in the darkness. Sloane managed to position himself so he was in front of Abby. As he inched along, he scanned the windows anxiously, but could detect no glimmer of light or any other sign of Connie's presence. Maybe she had already left.

There was no moon, and the lights lining the runway provided little illumination. The still night air hung around them, and Sloane heard his breath, ragged with tension, cutting through the darkness.

At last they reached the door of Abby's office. At her nod, Sloane felt for the knob and tried to turn it. It was locked. Sloane strained his ears but could hear no sound from inside.

Had Connie gone, or was she hidden inside, waiting for her chance to escape? In case she wasn't even aware of their presence, Sloane "tripped" over a slab of broken concrete and fell against the door, rattling it noisily.

An angry frown whipped across Abby's face and she raised her finger to her lips. Sloane shrugged his shoulders apologetically. Still miffed, Abby pulled her keys from her pocket and unlocked the door.

Sloane pushed the door open with agonizing slowness and, with Abby close on his heels, crept inside.

"Does everything look okay?" whispered Sloane.

"As far as I can tell in the dark," Abby returned. "Let me turn on the lights."

There was a click and then light flooded the room. Sloane peered around the small, barren office, receiving a stark impression of gray. Gray concrete floor, gray aluminum walls, gray metal desk and file cabinet. Abby evidently didn't see any need to brighten up her workplace; it was a strictly utilitarian room. His eye caught on a row of framed documents on the wall over the desk, a varied assortment of awards and certificates Abby had earned in her flying career. Those and a picture of Adam tucked away on a corner of the desk were the only personal items in evidence.

Sloane looked at the jumbled array of papers on the

desk and hoped that the disorder was a normal state of affairs and not the result of Connie's search. His hopes were dashed by a sharp exclamation from Abby.

"My files!" she cried in a choked voice.

Sloane followed her gaze to the back corner of the room. His heart sank at the sight of an open file drawer with a pile of folders resting on top. Connie must have been interrupted in mid-search.

Abby stepped over to the files, her eyes frantically scanning the papers. Sloane caught her outstretched arm in an iron grasp.

"Don't" he warned, his eyes curiously intent. "We shouldn't touch anything. Fingerprints, you know."

Abby stopped and pulled at her hair in frustration. Much as she wanted to check her files to find some clue as to what the intruder was searching for, she recognized the wisdom in what Sloane had said. Her gaze traversed the room and caught on a door in the corner.

Sloane followed her look and swallowed hard. Connie was no doubt hiding behind that door. Somehow he had to keep Abby from charging through it. His hand fell upon her shoulder, his heart jumping at the feel of her warm flesh beneath her shirt.

He held up his cell phone. "Let's call the police." He spoke in a harsh whisper, his eyes holding hers, compelling her to keep away from that door.

Abby shot him a withering glance. "You call the police if you want. I've got to go in and make sure my plane is okay." She set her chin in a stubborn line and tossed her blonde head defiantly.

With a sigh of exasperation, Sloane followed her through the door. His hand closed over hers as she reached for the light switch, and he shook his head warningly. Abby nodded to show she understood.

Sloane heard a slight rustle to his left. Quickly he pointed Abby to the right and by gestures, indicated that they should separate and meet on the other side of the hangar. With a slight shuffle, Abby moved off.

The huge DC-3 filled the entire hangar, looming ominously over Sloane as he inched his way along the wall. He paused under the wing and peered through the darkness. There was a flicker of movement along the wall and then a shadow as he passed by a hidden recess. He held himself rigidly, determined not to make any sound that would bring Abby over to investigate.

He continued circling the plane till he reached the other side of the hangar. Abby stood at the nose of the plane, her upraised arm leaning against it as she watched him.

"Not a thing," Sloane said in an unnaturally loud

voice to cover any noise Connie might make. "Now let's call the police." He put his hands on Abby's shoulders to turn her back the way she had come, but she solidly resisted his pressure, groping on the wall for another light switch. Suddenly the hangar was swathed in light, and Sloane shut his eyes against the glare.

"I've got to check my plane first and make sure it's okay," Abby said in a voice that Sloane was beginning to recognize all too well. He could only hope that he had given Connie enough of an opportunity to sneak out of the hangar. He waited impatiently, shifting from one foot to the other, while Abby examined her aircraft. At last she turned, an expression of uneasy relief on her face. "It's okay," she said. "There doesn't appear to be any damage."

"The police?" Sloane prompted, his voice smooth but insistent.

"Yes. Go ahead and call." Abby pivoted and strode quickly out of the hangar.

Sloane checked his long stride to match her own. Once out of the hangar, she pulled her own cell phone out of her pocket and called the police. As she made her phone call, a sudden thought struck Sloane and he contemplated it curiously. While true that Abby had not been in any great hurry to call the police, she had not protested too much either. Surprising for a drug dealer who should, by rights, wish to have as little to do with the police as possible. Obviously she didn't keep any incriminating evidence at the airport; otherwise she certainly wouldn't let the police poke around her office. He smothered a grin at the thought of Connie's reaction to what must have been a fruitless search. She was well known throughout the agency for her fierce temper.

Abby closed her cell phone, interrupting his thoughts. "They're on their way," she said shortly. While Sloane leaned casually against the outside wall of the hangar, Abby paced back and forth in front of her office, waiting for the police.

With a start, Sloane realized that underneath the loose knit of her shirt she was not wearing a bra. In the light provided by a nearby security light, he could clearly see the rounded globes of her breasts, and see the dark shadows of her nipples taut against the thick fabric. He felt a lurch of excitement within him, and his fingers ached to reach over and touch her. He made no attempt to hide the fact that he was watching her. Still, caught up in her own confused and angry thoughts, it took Abby a few moments to become aware of his intense interest. Sloane watched with amusement as a pale pink suddenly flooded her cheeks. She blushed so easily; it was very endearing. She lowered her eyes in momentary shyness and from deep inside dredged the words, "I had just stepped out of the shower when the phone rang."

Sloane's smile deepened, his broad shoulders heaving as he laughed. "You look much better after a shower than I do."

The air between them crackled with their mutual attraction. Abby took a step backward and tore her gaze away from his, more than a little disturbed at the sudden intensity of the conversation. The shrill shriek of the police siren tore through the night, and with a sense of relief, Abby turned away to meet the police, sending up a silent prayer of thanks for their timely intervention.

She quickly gave the two police officers all the information. They assiduously took notes and then moved inside the office. Since nothing seemed to have been stolen they declined to check for fingerprints. Under their direction, Abby checked through her files, but nothing was missing. The police politely hinted that Abby might have left the files out herself and left, without holding out much assurance that the culprit would ever be found. They promised Abby that they would investigate, but she knew full well that her mysterious break in was consigned to become another ignored report at an overworked police station.

Abby stood outside as the police drove away. The

tiny airport, which had always been such a friendly place, suddenly seemed sinister and menacing. Her office had been invaded, her private files exposed to a stranger's eyes. Why anyone would be interested in fuel consumption reports and cargo manifests, she didn't know, but they were hers and nobody else's business. All the events of the past few days welled up inside of her, and tears slowly found their way down her cheeks. Sloane came up silently behind her and, placing his hands on her shoulders, swung her around to face him. "Are you okay, Abby?" His eyes were filled with warmth and compassion.

Abby closed her eyes and lowered her head, not wanting him to see her cry. "Yes, I'm fine. It's just," her hands clenched into tiny balls at her sides and her lower lip trembled. "Someone was in here, going through my things, and I don't even know why!"

A momentary look of discomfort crossed Sloane's face, and Abby tried to pull herself away, realizing that her tears must be embarrassing to him. "I'm sorry, Sloane. You've been so kind, and here I just go to pieces on you." She pasted a tremulous smile on her lips.

Sloane desperately wanted to gather her into his arms and wipe away her tears. "You have no need to apologize," he murmured. "You've had a terrible shock; you have every right to be upset." Inside he wrestled with his own feelings of guilt. He and Connie had brought this distress upon her. Standing there, faced with her tears, it was easy to forget that she was a suspected drug dealer. All he could see when he looked at her was a frightened and vulnerable woman. He massaged her shoulder gently, wishing he knew what to say to put the sparkle back in her eyes.

His words unleashed something within her, and Abby yielded to the hot tears that coursed down her cheeks. Sloane forgot all about his charade of a marriage, forgot everything except easing the distress of the woman in front of him, and enfolded her in his arms.

She buried her face against the corded muscles of his chest, her tears flowing unchecked as he rocked her comfortingly back and forth, his strong hands patting her gently, his arms wrapped around her like a warm blanket. Abby clung to him. At last her tears stopped. Sloane's hand moved to brush the hair out of her face, and his touch was almost unbearable in its tenderness. His breath was warm and moist against her skin, and Abby became aware of just how closely their bodies were pressed together. His gaze traveled over her face as he searched her eyes. Something intense flared through his entrancement. For a moment, Sloane forgot everything, forgot who he was and the role he was being forced to play. For a moment the woman in his arms was just a woman and not a suspect. Then something clicked in his mind, and he realized how close he was to kissing her. A shudder of revulsion swept through him and he thrust her away.

Mortification swept over Abby as she realized what she had almost done. She saw the revulsion in his eyes and turned away. "I'm sorry!" she said in a wounded voice. It had been so long since she had been held in a man's arms, she thought.

"So am I," Sloane replied tautly, his jaw set in an unyielding line.

"We'd better get back home." Abby carefully avoided looking at his eyes. Once again, her emotions waged war inside of her, and she sought to erect a wall of defense against him.

"Yes." Sloane led the way to the car, his movements stiff and awkward. They rode back to the duplex in a long, brittle silence. Abby's hands gripped the steering wheel tightly, her mouth a straight line, her eyes looking firmly ahead as she mentally warned herself against letting herself be mesmerized by Sloane's charms ever again. As soon as she had parked the car, she spoke in a flat, impersonal tone. "Thanks, Sloane. I really appreciate your help."

Sloane touched her arm, making her flinch. "It was no problem," he said with quiet emphasis.

"I'm sure Connie must be worried about you," Abby replied through stiff lips.

For some reason her words seemed to amuse him. With a choking couch he replied, "Yeah, I suppose you're right." A smile crossed his face that went a long way toward dispelling the tension between them. For a moment it seemed as though he had something more to say, then he leaped out of the car and strode to his side of the duplex, hands jammed into his pockets, whistling softly. Abby remained in the car for a long moment, trying to sort through the events of the past few hours and put everything in perspective. "Friendly," she told herself. "He's just being friendly." She was reading way too much into what must have been a kind, neighborly act. With a firm shake of her head, she pushed all thoughts of Sloane out of her mind and went into her side of the duplex.

"Of all the miserable, idiotic bad luck!" Connie raged as she threw a pillow across the room. "I search high and low and don't find a blessed thing! Then some yahoo fly-boy sees my flashlight, so I almost get my cover blown!" Connie slammed her fist against the wall, shaking the framed pictures and knocking them askew.

"Yeah, Abby nearly nailed you there," said Sloane

with an unconcerned smile on his face. He held her cell phone in his hands and was manipulating the settings. He knew how to handle Connie's outbursts. He'd had enough experience, after all.

Connie shot him a furious look, followed by another pillow, which he easily ducked. "Wonder where she keeps her blasted files anyway!" she fumed. "I sure couldn't find them. I just came off looking like an idiot, that's all!"

"Tell you what. You don't mention my extra thorough search of Abby's lingerie, and I won't mention your highly effective use of the flashlight as a signaling tool," Sloane offered.

Connie glared at Sloane for a moment longer. Then her face and body relaxed, and she chuckled along with him. That was the good thing about Connie. She never stayed mad for long.

When Sloane stepped outside the next morning to pick up the paper, he saw with surprise that Abby, dressed in blue jeans and a denim shirt, was curled up like a blue ball on her porch. For a moment he thought she was asleep, but as he closed the door behind him, she unfolded and walked over to meet him. Her face was pale and pinched and her voice was hoarse with exhaustion.

"You look tired," Sloane said. "Didn't you get any sleep at all?"

Abby shook her head. "Not much." Her eyes sought his. "I just wanted to apologize."

"I thought you did that last night," Sloane reminded her.

Abby's cheeks burned in remembrance. She took a deep breath. "I'm sorry I got you in trouble with Connie. I couldn't help but hear you fighting after we got back. I just wanted to say I was sorry, and see if there was anything I could do to help." She squirmed uncomfortably under his intense gaze.

She must have heard Connie's temper tantrum, thought Sloane as he wondered how best to respond. He finally chose a casual approach. "Don't worry about it Abby," he grimaced in good humor. "Connie's mostly bark and no bite. She'll get over it."

"Well, I'm still sorry. You went to a lot of effort for me last night, and I'd hate to think you got into trouble on my account." Two deep lines of worry appeared between her large green eyes.

Sloane hesitated. Normally he would launch into his martyred spiel about how his wife didn't understand him, but he was reluctant to try that line on Abby. She was much too smart to fall for that, he told himself. He settled for a less hackneyed response. "Connie's got problems that have nothing to do with you," he said, allowing his shoulders to slump just a little. He put a note of wistfulness in his tone as he added, "Sometimes you just don't learn what someone's really like until after the wedding."

Sloane fell into a calculated silence during which he tried to gauge Abby's reaction. The intensity of her response took him by surprise. She stared back at him with stained eyes. "And sometimes not even then," she finally murmured. With that, she turned and fled into her duplex.

Sloane stared after her with a bemused expression on his face. He ought to get an award for his great acting ability, he thought, resolutely pushing out of his mind the thought that he had not been acting when he'd held Abby Tarleton in his arms the night before.

CHAPTER FIVE

Sloane hummed slightly as he finished shaving and glanced out the window. A small figure outside caught his interest. "I'm going out back to chat up the kid, Con," he called.

Connie sat at the table, glancing through some reports with a frown on her face. She looked up. "The way to Mom's heart is through the kid, eh?"

"Something like that." Sloane finished buttoning his checkered work shirt and went outside where Abby's son sat in his sandbox, filling a pail with slightly damp sand. His face was already grubby, and a lock of hair the same strawberry blonde as Abby's fell across his forehead.

Sloane admired the fine lines of the large wooden sandbox, much sturdier than the ones in stores. Out of the corner of his eye he caught a glimpse of Abby standing in the kitchen window, watching them. He waved at her, hoping she was not still upset about what had happened between them the night before. He was relieved when she waved back in a friendly manner and moved away from the window. "Nice sandbox," Sloane commented to Adam.

"Uh-huh," Adam responded, intent on his play.

"Did you make it?"

“No!” A ready smile, reminiscent of Abby’s crossed the little boy’s face. “My Uncle Ned did.”

“Wow! He does good work. Did you help?”

“Uh-huh,” Adam’s eyes shone with pride. “I got to hammer in four nails.”

“Which ones?” Sloane crouched and closely scrutinized the nails.

“One at each corner,” Adam replied gravely. “That one, that one, that one, and that one.”

“Very nice job!” The warmth of Sloane’s smile echoed in his voice.

“Wanna play?”

“Sure! What are you doing?” Sloane bent his head to the task. When Abby stepped out thirty minutes later, he and Adam had a huge city built, complete with airport, of course.

Abby held a pitcher of lemonade and some glasses. “Time for a break?” she asked, giving Sloane a conspiratorial wink.

Sloane let out a long, audible breath. His heart quickened at the sight of her in beige shorts and cream-colored, sleeveless shirt. Even though the Texas sun was well on its way to heating up the morning, and Sloane felt beaded drops of sweat on his own forehead, she looked cool and fresh. All traces of her earlier tormented state had vanished. There was a soft color in her temptingly curved mouth and her hair tumbled carelessly down her back, the first time he had seen it unrestrained.

Adam eagerly reached for his lemonade and took it to the swing set to drink on the top of the slide. Abby settled on the steps of the back porch and with a tip of her head, motioned for Sloane to sit beside her. He dropped down and saw by the flicker of her eyes that he was closer than she had intended. He reached for the glass of the sparkling lemonade, a faint glint of humor in his eyes. His hand closed over hers as he took the glass, his fingers cool and smooth against her skin.

Abby pulled her hand away. She raised her eyes to his, intrigued by the challenge she saw therein. Abby's brow furrowed, perplexed. Was she just imagining things? No, the almost electrical attraction between them was obvious. She knew he was aware of it too, but they seemed to have made an unspoken pact not to talk about it. It was sheer torture, however, to sit next to Sloane and attempt to carry on an ordinary conversation with him. Abby looked pensively into her lemonade glass, swirling the ice cubes inside before taking a deep, cooling draught.

Sloane raised his glass to her. "Thanks."

"Thanks for playing with Adam," Abby said quickly over her choking, beating heart. "All his friends are gone right now and he's been rather lonely." She took a long sip and ran her tongue along her lips, savoring the tart sweetness of the lemonade.

Sloane caressed his glass idly between his hands. "You're not flying today?"

"I have a flight tonight." Abby shifted her body a fraction of an inch away from him so she wouldn't be quite so aware of his bare thigh pressed against hers.

"Who watches Adam while you're flying?" Sloane leaned back, locked his hands behind his head, and stretched his long legs casually before him.

"I have a woman a couple blocks over. She has two little boys of her own, and doesn't have a problem with my irregular hours."

Abby forced her voice to remain calm and steady. She didn't want him to know how much he was affecting her.

"That's good." Sloane looked at her enigmatically. "I don't know many women pilots. Particularly not many who fly freight."

"I don't know of any others out at this airport,

although I know there are some at Meacham."

"How did you get into flying?"

A smile touched Abby's lips. "My stepfather was a pilot. He taught me how to fly. I grew up in a house filled with planes. We built models together, went to air shows together. I was the son he-" she bit her lip.

"What?" Sloane's voice was unbelievably gentle.

"The son he always wished Ned would be." Abby stared morosely in front of her, the heel of her sandal scuffing aimlessly in the dirt at her feet.

"Sounds like a good man."

Again, gentleness. Abby was surprised and touched. "He was a very good man," Abby lifted her chin determinedly. "I always wished he could have been my real dad. He wanted to adopt me, but my father wouldn't let him. Don't know why." She made a wry face. "He never had anything else to do with me." Her head bowed and she remained in an attitude of frozen stillness. Actually, she did know why.

Her father, a strict army officer, had been an extremely possessive man. Anything he touched or had contact with had to be his and his only, whether it was things or people. After years of denying unfounded accusations about other men, Abby's mother had left him. Or so she thought. Abby's father tracked them down, forcibly dragged them back home with them, and dared her mother to leave again. Somehow Abby's mother had dredged up the courage to file for divorce, facing threats of violence from her husband every step of the way. For a while Abby's mother had refused to let her daughter out of her sight for fear her father might try to kidnap her. Gradually, though, those restrictions had eased and disappeared as her father, in unforgiving hatred, cast his wife and daughter completely out of his life.

Perhaps that was why she valued her independence so much. Why she insisted on running her own business instead of being a cog in someone else's. Her father, unwittingly, had made her value her freedom. Her stepfather had given her his love of flying and of life.

Abby finished her lemonade, setting the glass behind her on the porch. She drew her knees up, hugging them to her. For the moment, she forgot about the man beside her and lost herself in her memories.

Sloane watched her with concern. What was going through her mind, he wondered. What demons had he disturbed? Part of him wanted to back off, to leave her alone with her thoughts, but the detective part of him knew that he couldn't. He had to take every opportunity to chip away at her facade and uncover the secrets within. With a gentle nudge, he brought her back from her daydreams. "Is your stepfather still alive?"

"No. He died of a heart attack several years ago. My mother died soon after." Abby closed her eyes, and left unspoken the fact that her stepfather had died after learning that Ned had been arrested for dealing in drugs. Ned and the dashing young pilot he had introduced Abby to. Joe Tarleton.

Adam ran up and handed his mother his sand-covered lemonade glass, then ran back to the sandbox to continue his work on his city, his face a sticky mess of lemonade and sand. Abby held his glass idly in her hands, her expression unreadable.

Sloane took a look at her whitened knuckles clenched around the glass. A chord struck deep inside of him and he stirred uneasily, shifting his body away from hers. Job be damned, he wouldn't be able to live with himself if he pushed her any more just now. He nodded at Adam. "He's quite a boy. Looks a lot like you."

"Yes." Abby's tone was still guarded, her eyes still veiled. She swallowed hard.

Sloane took a deep breath. His hand reached out and stopped, just inches away from her face. He longed to stroke her cheek, to put his arm around her and hold her. His hand hovered and then dropped to his knee. He had a job to do, and Abby deserved no mercy. Forcing an image of his brother lying cold on his deathbed to the front of his mind, Sloane took a deep breath and spoke, the words grating like gravel across his throat. "Does he ever see his father?" He waited for her response, but if he was hoping for a reaction of any kind, he was disappointed. Abby abruptly regained her self-control and deflected his question with a chuckle.

"This sounds an awful lot like an interview, Mr. Jameson." She cocked her head and regarded him out of the corner of her eye. A smile twitched at the corners of her mouth, a glint of her usual good humor finally returning.

Sloane shook his head. His mouth spread in a thin-lipped smile. "Sorry," he said in an odd tone. "Force of habit. I still would like to do a story about you though."

"No. But thank you anyway." Abby smiled to soften the blow. The door next door slammed, and Connie came out to stand next to them, dressed, as usual, in a business-like suit. Abby offered her a friendly smile. "You look hot," she said with sympathy. "Would you like a glass of lemonade?"

"No thanks," Connie replied. "I'm on my way to work. I just came out to see if you needed anything at the store, Sloane. I'll stop and pick up some odds and ends on my way home this evening."

"Can't think of anything, Con." Sloane leaned back

and grinned up at his “wife”. "Have a good day." He cocked his head at Abby. "Can you believe it, Connie? Abby won't let me do a story about her!" His face was a study in wounded indignation.

"But I was just about to offer to take him up in a small plane," Abby said hurriedly. "Both of you, of course." Her smile included Connie. As soon as the words were out, Abby regretted them. She was afraid of having too much to do with Sloane Jameson, afraid that her own rapidly growing feelings for him would cause her to do something she would regret. She held her breath, hoping he and Connie would decline her offer, but no such luck.

"Yes, I would like that very much." There was an eagerness in his eyes that gratified her even as it filled her with dismay. He turned and looked expectantly at Connie, but the other woman was shaking her head with a slight shudder.

"Not a chance!" she said with her pert nose wrinkled in distaste. "I hate planes!" She swiveled on her spike heels. "I've got to go now. Bye!"

"Bye," Abby waved. She turned back to Sloane. "All right. I'll set up a time and let you know. Maybe tomorrow?" She raised her eyebrows questioningly.

Sloane nodded. "That would be great. I'll look forward to it." He stood up and dusted off his shorts. For a moment he stood over her, his hands planted firmly on his hips. His glittering eyes bore deep into hers, and she stared back, unblinking, fascinated, and a little frightened by what she saw in them. Then he looked abruptly away.

"Thanks for the lemonade. See you later." He covered the ground to his own back door in four long, easy steps, the screen door slamming in a jarring, final note.

Abby heard the harsh ring of the telephone from inside. She pulled herself up and stepped into the kitchen. "Hello?" She stiffened as she heard a familiar growl at the other end.

"Yeah. Double me again. Same place."

Abby dropped the phone like a hot potato, and then called Adam inside. It was time to do something about those phone calls. In the next hour, she tried four times to call the phone company, but the line was busy each time. Finally she decided to stop in on her way to the police station. It would probably be better to take care of the matter in person anyway.

The woman at the phone company was very pleasant as she entered the work order into her computer. "It will take three to five days for your new number to be connected," she said in a chatty tone. "We'll call when it happens to make sure the transfer went okay. Do you want a recording on your old line giving the new number?"

"No!" Abby said more sharply than she intended. "Someone's got a hold of my number by mistake," she explained. "That's why I'm changing my number. And I'd like the new number unlisted, please," she added.

"All right. I'll get this order put in right away for you."

"Thank you. Come on, Adam." Abby stood up and, swinging the boy's hand gently, left the phone company and walked across the street to the police station. After a few minutes, she was ushered to a seat in a bustling office where a harried looking detective gave a low whistle at the sight of the money that Abby laid before him. He scratched his curly head in perplexity.

"You say the guy just tossed the money at you and drove off? That doesn't make sense!"

"I know," Abby agreed. "That's why I came to you."

The detective shook his head. "Would you know the guy if you saw him again?"

"Definitely," Abby said. She'd recognize that big nose anywhere.

"Do you have time to look through some photos to see if you can pick him out?"

Abby glanced at Adam who fidgeted in his chair and shook her head regretfully. "No. I'd better come back sometime when I don't have him with me."

The detective nodded, not really concerned. "Well, I'll put the money in the safe here and see what I can find out. Of course, if no one claims it, it's yours.

Abby shivered. "I don't want it," she said with conviction. "I have a feeling that it's dirty money, and I don't want any part of it."

The detective eyed her cynically. "Well, if you change your mind, you know where it is."

Abby grabbed Adam's hand and left, wondering why she didn't feel more relieved now that the money was out of her hands. A vague sense of disquiet nagged at the back of her mind and somehow she had a feeling that the strange game in which she was inexplicably involved was not finished playing.

CHAPTER SIX

Abby smiled comfortably at Sloane as he slid into the passenger seat of her two-door car, his hair brushing against the roof over his head. "You ready?" she asked. Her low voice held a hint of challenge.

Sloane nodded a yes. His blue eyes deepened as they looked across at her, and she flushed a tad under his gaze. She had to admit that she'd taken just a little more care than usual over her appearance that morning. She wore her usual blue jeans, but had picked her newest pair and instead of her usual t-shirt, wore a cream-colored polo shirt. Loose tendrils of golden hair fluttered around her face. She'd gathered it up into her usual ponytail, but she'd added a touch of make-up, which she usually abhorred.

"You'll have to roll down the window," Abby said as she swung the car out into the street. "The air conditioner's broken. Needs a new compressor."

"Ouch! That's expensive."

"Yes. I'd hoped to have enough to get it fixed before summer hit but didn't quite make it." Adam had fallen and cut his head, requiring several stitches at the local emergency room. Abby repressed a shudder just thinking of it.

As they approached the airport, Abby reminded herself that today she would keep her relationship with Sloane on a strictly friendly basis. She had no intention of permitting herself to fall under his spell again. He was married, and whatever his feelings for her, or hers for him, that fact obviated anything they might possibly have between them, no matter how intense.

Sloane was too distracted to notice Abby's new air of resolve. He wondered why she couldn't afford to get her car fixed. Surely a drug dealer who was as high up in the scheme of things as he suspected Abby might be wouldn't turn a hair at paying for a car repair. Yet he and Connie had noted that Abby did live very modestly. She must be hiding the money somewhere. Just like everything else.

At the airport, Sloane stopped for a moment behind the chain link fence that separated the grass from the paved parking area for the aircraft while Abby walked on toward the plane. He stood and watched, legs planted firmly apart, arms akimbo, as Abby went through her preflight check of the aircraft she would be flying, a blue and white Cessna 150.

Sloane was filled with a sense of anticipation, like a

schoolboy about to go on his first date. He looked forward to another chance to be alone with Abby, and to his surprise, it wasn't just because he might get some information about her drug-related activities. He found that the more time he spent with Abby, the more he was attracted to her. Always before when on assignment, he had been able to keep his purpose at the forefront of his mind. With Abby, he was finding that next to impossible, and he knew that he was in danger of losing his objectivity over her. He'd met drug dealers he'd liked before, but never before had he felt such a reluctance to carry out his assignment, to perform the prodding and goading that was required of someone in his position.

Abby's slim figure was snugly outlined by her jeans as she bent over to check the fuel. The bright sun that put everything else in sharp relief, only accentuated the red highlights of her hair. Sloane's mouth curved into an unconscious smile as he watched her. Yes, he would definitely have to watch his objectivity on this case. How could such a lively person as Abby be involved in the sordid world of drugs? It just didn't seem possible that this woman, who obviously had such love for her own son, was involved in an industry which resulted in the death of thousands of sons and daughters yearly. Once again the familiar features of his brother formed in his mind, features very similar to his own, reminding him of his duty.

With a shake of his head, Sloane put all that out of his mind and walked through the gate onto the pavement. Abby, just finishing her preflight check as Sloane approached, turned around. As her eyes met his, she thought she saw a flicker of anger in them, then he came closer, and she decided she must have been mistaken. Why should he be angry with her? A ready smile crossed her face, and she teased lightly, "I thought you'd come up when I finished. Why wait? Afraid I'd put you to work?"

Sloane rewarded her with a smile of his own. "No. I was just admiring your plane." He paused; then the words came out in a rush before he even realized what he was going to say. "And its pilot."

Abby's smile slipped a moment. She seized on his first comment and said wistfully, "Not my airplane, I'm afraid. The only one I have is the DC-3 I fly freight in. This one belongs to a friend of mine. He lets me borrow it every now and then. Maybe someday I'll have one of my own." Her hand trailed along the side of the plane. Her stepfather's beloved Waco Biplane had been sold to meet Ned's legal expenses. She swiveled quickly, turning her back, and busied herself going over yet another preflight checklist.

At last she was satisfied that the plane was safe and

swung into the cockpit. Sloane settled down in the seat beside her. Abby spent a moment checking her instruments, and then she turned to show Sloane how to fasten his safety belt. She bent over him to help fasten the strap, her face hovering over his. As she started to draw back, he placed a restraining hand on her arm. His fingers reached out to touch her cheek in a wistful gesture, then traced the outline of her lips. Abby closed her eyes and let out a long, drawn out sigh. His mouth slowly reached up to hers. The touch of his lips was a delicious sensation, and Abby was shocked by her own eager response, but not so shocked that she lost sight of whom she was kissing. With an abrupt shove, she pushed herself away from him.

"Let's get something straight right now," she said, her eyes level with his, her voice even. "I do not get involved with married men. If you can't keep our relationship on a friendly level, then you need to get out now."

"I'm sorry," he said contritely.

Abby's expression almost softened at the sight of his anguished face.

"I'm sorry," he repeated. For a flitting moment, Sloane bitterly resented the deception he and Connie had been forced to practice upon Abby. More than anything he wanted to lean over, to sample one more taste of her sweet lips. With a shudder, he closed his eyes and forced himself to fall back into his role as Connie's husband. "Please forgive me," he whispered.

Abby nodded with a taut jerk of her head. Sloane reached out and clutched at her hand. "Please," he said hoarsely. Unspoken pain was alive and glowing in his eyes. "I can't bear to have you think what you must be thinking of me. Hell, yes, I'm attracted to you! But I love Connie, and I've never cheated on her." He shook his head, his eyes falling to the floor. "I don't know what got into me just now. I won't let it happen again. I promise!"

For a long moment she looked back at him. Then she smoothed her brow with both hands. "All right." Her voice was still guarded, but friendlier.

Sloane struggled to keep a casual note in his voice. The encounter had shaken him more than he cared to admit. Talk about her, he told himself. Talk about flying. Get that look off her face somehow. "You could probably make a lot more money flying for an airline," he commented.

"Probably," Abby nodded. "But I'd fly a lot more hours, be tied to the schedule they set for me, and a computer would be doing most of my work. Flying freight, I set my own schedule mostly, and I'm not putting my life in anyone else's hands. And there's one other benefit," she admitted with a half laugh.

"What's that?" Sloane raised his eyebrows inquiringly.

"I don't have to put up with any passengers!" Abby chuckled as she glanced at him out of the corner of her eye.

Sloane was glad that they were back on a friendly footing, "Sometimes I can see where that might be an advantage," he agreed, thinking of some of the boorish passengers that had been on some of his flights. "I'm surprised you agreed to take me up."

Abby taxied the plane out onto the runway. "So am I. I don't usually take anyone but Adam, and occasionally Ned. But you don't seem too obnoxious."

"Thanks, I think." For a moment all conversation stopped while Abby went through her final take-off checks--throttle and flaps, and called the tower for clearance. Then they were racing down the runway. Sloane had flown in airliners before, but never in a small aircraft. There was a world of difference between the two. Now he felt the power of the plane as it lifted off the runway and into the sky. The sensation of flying was much more intense and real.

For the first few minutes the vibrations and movements of the airplane made him feel slightly queasy, but then that feeling was left behind as he was caught up in the excitement of being high enough to see the world, but not so high as to see only the tops of clouds. He could look straight down with no wing obstructing his view, the Cessna's wing being placed sensibly on top of the aircraft.

He looked at Abby to find her watching him. Her eyes sparkled as she shared his delight. They exchanged smiles. "My world and welcome to it," she said. "Would you like to see our duplex?"

"Sure," Sloane had to raise his voice to be heard over the noise of the engine.

Abby's smile took on a mischievous aspect. "Okay." Without warning, the plane tipped on its side as Sloane clutched at the edge of his seat. The wing on his side seemed to point straight down, fixed on one point in the air as the rest of the plane few in a circle around it.

"That's it, just at the end of the wing," Abby said, keeping any trace of laughter at Sloane's surprise and discomfort from her voice, but not from her eyes.

Looking down, it took him a few moments to recognize it. Seeing it from above was just not normal, but then he recognized the elementary school that was four blocks away and suddenly the pattern of streets and houses became familiar. "Yes. I see it now!"

Abby laughed gently as she righted the plane. Glancing over at him, she said, "Sorry. I just couldn't resist. Mean streak, I guess. And besides, it pays you back for being so darned attractive."

Sloane's smile deepened into laughter. "You know, once I got used to it, it was fun. All of this is so much more enjoyable than being buried in an airliner."

A devilish glint came into her eyes. "Oh? Then you're ready for me to do a loop then?"

"No!" Sloane grimaced in good humor as he held his hands in front of him in mock supplication and protest. "Have pity on me this time out!"

Abby put on a serious expression for a moment before replying with an exaggerated sigh. "Okay. But I was really looking forward to doing some snap rolls, loops, and hammerheads. Spoilsport!" Her lower lip jutted out in a pout.

"Let me get used to this first, please. Maybe next time or the time after."

Abby shook her head. "Couldn't do all of those in this airplane anyway. Have to borrow someone else's plane for those tricks. If you're interested."

Sloane regarded her curiously. "You really know acrobatics?"

"Sure. I was on my college acrobatics team," Abby said with an adventurous toss of her head.

"Really? Were you any good?"

Shaking her head, Abby said, "I didn't set the sky on fire or anything, but I was pretty good. My team one the show more often than not."

"I'm impressed," Sloane said with a significant lift of his eyebrow. "Do you still do acrobatic flying?"

"No. I'm way too busy tending my business and Adam." There was a trace of longing in Abby's voice as she continued. "Too many responsibilities and not enough time, or money. Everyone's complaint nowadays."

Sloane nodded thoughtfully. The conversation was much too causal. Time to push her a little. "And you also have to take care of Ned," he said.

Abby looked surprised for a moment. "Ned? Oh, he doesn't live with me. He's just there temporarily. No more than a week, I hope." Abby hesitated and then added, "Ned's got a few problems. He means well, but he just can't stay away from the wrong type of friends. Still, Adam adores him and he is my stepbrother."

"Maybe he'll straighten out. What is he, early twenties? Kids often go through a rough stage about then. My brother did." Sloane wished he could take the words back as soon as he said them. What was it about her anyway? He didn't like to talk about Scott to anybody.

"Oh? Did he straighten out?" Abby noted the change in Sloane's voice and kept her voice soft.

"He didn't have a chance." Pain flitted across Sloane's face. "He died of a drug overdose when he was twenty." Although the pain in his heart became a sick, fiery gnawing, he watched Abby carefully to see her reaction. Might as well get some use out of this since he'd brought it up.

"I'm sorry," Abby looked uncomfortable.

"Yeah," Sloane said. He didn't mean to go on but he did, in a hushed voice. "I worshipped him. Tagged along after him everywhere he went. Drove him absolutely crazy sometimes!"

Abby laughed.

"He just changed overnight," Sloane's eyes darkened with remembered pain. "He didn't have time for me anymore. I couldn't talk to him. No one could talk to him."

Abby nodded with a sense of familiarity. That was how it had been for her and Joe.

"Mom and Dad were worried, but I covered for him." Sloane snorted. "I loaned him money, made excuses for him. I'd've walked on water if he'd asked me to. I trusted him when he said he was okay." Sloane's voice trembled. Now that he had started talking about it, he couldn't have stopped if he'd wanted to. Abby let him talk, sensing that he needed to get this out.

"I knocked on his door one night. He didn't answer, so I pushed the door open." Sloane's voice dropped to a whisper. "He was on the bed. Dead."

Abby gasped involuntarily.

"The autopsy showed he died from drugs that were cut badly. They were too powerful." Sloane shook his head. "I've always blamed myself. If I had told my parents- he would still be alive."

"You don't know that," Abby said bluntly,

"I should have told them--"

"How old were you?"

"Eleven."

"You're putting an awful lot on an eleven-year-old boy," Abby said firmly, her eyes widening with certainty. "You can't blame yourself. Think of all the other people who should have been able to tell something was wrong. Your brother's teachers, your parents, all kinds of people. And face it, Sloane; drug habits aren't easy to break. Your brother wouldn't have been able to stop unless he wanted to. No one else could have made him stop."

Listening to her, Sloane knew she was right, but he couldn't let go of the guilt and anger he'd felt when he discovered his brother's body. Those feelings had carried him into undercover work, had helped to give him a mission in life. Whenever he put a drug dealer behind bars, he was keeping someone's older brother alive.

Abby cast a sidelong glance at his face. She could see that he was struggling to get his feelings under control.

Helpfully she changed the subject, giving him a few moments to compose himself. Quietly she drew his attention to some landmarks below. Sloane watched, enthralled, as she pointed out the highways and streets beneath them, the landmarks and tourist attractions such as Texas Stadium where the Dallas Cowboys played, the Ballpark in Arlington, home of the Texas Rangers baseball team, and the Six Flags over Texas amusement park. Even as he looked down, Sloane's mind was busy calculating what to do next. He hadn't meant to bare so much of his heart to Abby, but since he had, he might as well press the advantage. "Adam seems to have inherited your love of planes," he commented.

"He didn't have much choice. His father was a pilot." The words were out before Abby realized it.

"Oh? Does he fly freight too?"

"He did when I met him. I flew bush in Alaska after I got out of college. I came home for a visit, and Ned introduced us. After we got married, I stayed here to fly freight with him." Abby clenched the control stick with whitened knuckles. She hadn't talked so much about Joe in years.

"I'm surprised you didn't drag him back to fly bush with you."

A smile touched her lips. "I tried. It was so beautiful

up there. But Texas is home. And it's warmer in the winter. My bones didn't take the cold too well. Besides, my family was here. I'd always planned to raise my children near their grandparents. I wish they could have known Adam."

"When did they die?"

"A few months before he was born. Ned was arrested," Abby cast a glance in Sloane's direction. "For drug dealing. My stepfather couldn't take the shock. He died of a heart attack. My mother died soon after. I don't think I'll ever be able to forgive Ned for that."

"What about your husband?" Sloane pressed.

Abby swallowed hard. "I divorced him before Adam was born. He’s in prison serving a fifteen-year sentence. For drug smuggling."

"Does Adam know?"

"He knows his father is in jail for doing something very bad. When he's older, I'll tell him why."

"Do you have any contact with your ex at all?" Sloane pressed.

"No more than I can help. It wasn't hard to get total custody, and I gladly gave up any child support, not that he would be likely to ever provide it. He writes, occasionally. I keep his letters so Adam can have them someday. I don't think it would be fair to get rid of them without letting him ever see them. Other than that, no. I don't write to him, and we don't visit him. I don't really want Adam to have anything to do with him, and hope that by the time he's released from prison, Adam will have decided that for himself."

Looking at Abby, Sloane could detect no sign that she knew Joe was already out of prison. He briefly wondered if she ever played poker. He continued to press. "Why? Was your marriage that horrible?"

"No, not really," Abby said slowly, choosing her words carefully. "It just wasn't much of a marriage. I thought that our love of planes would be a starting point, but it was all we shared. It wasn't enough. He was involved with Ned and his friends, and I was sort of shut out of his life." Abby fell silent; a wry smile twisted her lips. "When he was arrested he tried to claim he was doing it for me and the baby. He should have known that I wouldn't have anything to do with that kind of money!"

Sloane studied her intently, looking for a hint of prevarication, but he couldn't find any. What a good liar she is, he thought admiringly. He could almost have believed her, if he didn't know otherwise. A tiny doubt about her involvement niggled at the back of his head, but he resolutely pushed it aside. Abby was involved. The evidence was just too strong to deny. Still, something just didn't make sense. Abby seemed completely sincere. Sloane shook his head. He couldn't figure it out. He would just have to hope that all would be made clear before long.

CHAPTER SEVEN

"You're crazy!" Connie snapped. "You go for one airplane ride with the woman, and come back with your judgment totally screwed up!"

"All I said was I was beginning to wonder whether or not she was really in on it, or if we were barking up the wrong tree," Sloane said patiently. "You didn't hear her, Con. She was genuinely angry at her ex and her stepbrother."

"Yeah, angry with them for getting caught," Connie said scathingly. "Boy, she's really conned you! Tell me," her voice lowered huskily. "Do you think you have a chance with her?"

Sloane flushed. "It was nothing like that-"

"Wasn't it? Come on, Sloane. We've been working on this case for months. Don't blow it now!" Connie tapped the sheath of papers on the table. "I've got it all here. Did you know that in every town she flies to there is a known member of the gang? Did you know that she turns down flights to places unless there is a gang member there?"

"Coincidence," Sloane said uncomfortably.

"There is no coincidence in our line of work. What about those phone calls? What about that money?" Connie turned away and took a few deep breaths to calm herself down. "Come on, Sloane. You've been at this as long as I have. You know what the score is. Now you've gone a fair way to working yourself into her confidence. Play it up. Get her to talk to you. Let's wrap this case up, so you and I can take a good, long vacation. We both could use a rest."

Sloane slammed out the back door. He stopped short at the sight of Abby sitting on her back porch, watching Adam on his swing set. She looked cool and fresh in a crisp, white linen skirt and a lime green sleeveless shirt that matched the sandals strapped around her fine-boned ankles. "Hi," she said in a mild, friendly voice. If she'd heard the fight between him and Connie, she gave no sign.

Sloane frowned, hating himself for what he was about to do. "Crazy woman, there's just no pleasing her sometimes!" he muttered under his breath as he ambled over and flung himself on the step beside her.

"Who? Connie?" Abby didn't let on that she'd heard the raised voices through the wall. She'd not been able to tell what they were saying, but she knew that both people were angry. She told herself that she should go inside and leave Sloane alone. The last thing she needed was to get mixed up in his marital problems. She poised to stand up, but Sloane's face forestalled her departure.

“Sometimes I think it was a mistake to get married," Sloane said calculatingly. "I mean for Connie and me. We're just too different. She's not the same anymore." He cocked an eye at her to gauge her reaction to this.

Abby tried to ignore the anguish in his voice, firmly resolving not to get involved in the situation. "It can be difficult sometimes," she said in a disinterested voice. "How long have you been married?"

"About a year. Things started off great, but lately it seems that all we do is fight." A muscle quivered at his jaw.

Abby studied his taut, drawn face and felt a stab of pain at her heart. Nevertheless, she forced herself to say in a passionless voice, "I'm sure it will be okay, Sloane. A lot of marriages go through this. It's sort of an adjustment period."

"Did yours?"

Abby chose her words carefully. "No. Joe was never around enough for us to fight." She bit her lip.

"Does it hurt? What he did to you?" His voice was tender, almost a murmur.

Abby shook her head. "He didn't really do anything to me. But my stepfather. He couldn't forgive Ned for introducing me to him. And he blamed himself for what happened to Ned, although I don't see how he could have changed things." Abby's voice trailed off into a heavy silence. She clamped her jaw tight and stared sightlessly into the distance.

"What about Ned now? Has he been able to keep his nose clean?" Sloane regarded her with a speculative gaze.

Abby shrugged. "I try not to wonder about it. I know he still has friends who are questionable. But I don't really want to know anymore than I have to."

Now Sloane's eyes peered at her with a curious intensity. "What about you? Has he ever tried to get you involved in anything?"

Abby's eyes took on a faraway look. "Once, many years ago. Before Joe. He asked me to fly a package somewhere. I refused. And that was the end of it. He knows how I feel about it." Something disturbing replaced Sloane's intense gaze, but Abby couldn't quite put a finger on it.

"If you suspect he's involved with something he shouldn't be, why don't you call the police?" His voice was carefully colored in neutral shades.

"I can't," Abby spoke with quiet, but desperate, firmness. "He is my brother."

"Your stepbrother," Sloane pointed out.

"My stepbrother. But I just can't turn him in. And, if

he gets into trouble with the police, I'll do everything I can to get him out of it." Her voice was final.

"Even if it's not the best thing for him?"

"It's what my stepfather would have wanted." Something flickered deep in Abby's eyes. "He was so proud of Ned. We all were. If only you'd known him then. He was so easy-going, so quick to make friends, made such good grades with so little effort. Everyone liked him. Everything was easy for Ned."

"And you resented that I bet," Sloane guessed.

"No, not at all," came Abby's quick reply. "I loved him too. It was impossible not to." Her lips parted in a gentle laugh. "You should have seen me then. I was thirteen. Shy, gawky, too tall and too skinny. I was scared to death when my mom remarried. I didn't really want another father, not after what I'd been through with my own dad, and not only was I getting a stepfather, but I was getting a stepbrother. I was terrified!"

Sloane laughed with her.

"He wasn't much to look at. He was three years younger than me, and small for his age. Just a scrawny little thing, but he had a way of filling the room. That first night at dinner I could barely swallow my food, but he was Mr. Personality, joking, laughing, teasing my mom like he was born to her. I just knew I'd knew I'd never fit in, never be able to talk to him or his dad the way he was talking to Mom." Abby hunched forward, resting her elbows on her knees and clasping her hands in front of her.

"He started right off, calling me 'sis'. But that bugged me more than anything. I wasn't his sister for pete's sake. Then I noticed how much he ate."

"A lot?" Sloane asked with a grin, remembering his own appetite as a teen-ager.

"He had five helpings of my mom's casserole! My mom was so thrilled that she'd pleased her new family. But I was suspicious because the thing is, my mom was a lousy cook. It was all a person could do to choke down one helping of her food, much less five."

Sloane's eyes crinkled in amusement.

"I'd heard that boys could eat anything but I couldn't believe that he could swallow that many helpings of Mom's cooking. So I watched him. He noticed me watching him and kind of grinned at me and winked. The food disappeared from his plate and I saw him looking down. I looked under the table and saw his dog, a big, huge mongrel, sitting across Ned's feet, wagging his tail and waiting for his next handout. I looked back at Ned and he winked at me again." Now Abby leaned back and stretched. "That night I joined Ned in the kitchen for a midnight snack. Ned and I both fed the rest of our meals to the dog and my mother went to her grave, firmly believing that we delighted in her home cooking."

A cloud passed across Abby's face suddenly. Sloane reached out to touch her arm. "You okay, Abby?"

Abby gave a quick start. "We were so happy then," she whispered. "And now it's all gone. My parents are dead. I've grown up and Ned...Ned hasn't. He's just careening through life, counting on his sense of humor and his personality to keep him out of trouble. And someday, someday he's going to dig himself in too deep and not be able to get back out." Abby's heart squeezed in anguish.

"Hey, it'll be okay," Sloane said, knowing even as he spoke that it wouldn't be okay.

Abby jerked to her feet and drew her tongue over her dry lips. She'd better get herself inside before she totally dissolved into tears in front of Sloane. He had enough problems of his own; he didn't need hers too. "Adam? It's time to go. Mommy has a flight tonight."

Sloane stared after her as she took the little boy inside with her. A jumble of confused thoughts assailed him. He could not comprehend his feelings for her, but he just could not reconcile the Abby he had just seen with the Abby that Connie insisted was involved with the drug ring.

Ned slouched into the fast food restaurant and looked around till he spotted Joe in the corner eating a sandwich. "What's going on, man?" Ned asked with a welcoming grin.

Joe waved Ned to a seat and took a long sip of his coke. Ned sat back and regarded his friend expectantly. He figured Joe wanted to ask about Abby. Instead the older man surprised Ned by stating, “We’ve got a snitch somewhere.”

Ned soared at Joe, his mouth wide open in surprise. “What are you talking about, Joe?”

Joe emptied his drink and sucked air through his straw. “We’ve got a snitch,” he repeated impatiently.

“How do you know?”

“I just know! Too many arrests. Too many people getting caught that shouldn’t.” He reached into his pocket and pulled out a scrap of paper that he shoved across the table.

Ned picked it up and looked at it questioningly. “What’s this?”

“It’s a list of all the dealers we’ve lost in the last few weeks.”

Ned whistled. “Quite a few.”

“Too many!” Joe snapped.

Ned looked at the paper again. “What are the

numbers by the names?"

"That's the amount of stuff they had with them when they were picked up." Joe slammed his fist on the table. "I wanna find out who the snitch is! And when I do-"

Ned shuddered inwardly. He didn't need to hear any more. He was very much aware of how violent Joe could be.

Joe brooded for a few moments and then looked up. "How's my wife?" he asked abruptly.

Ned looked intently at his friend. "You're divorced, Joe."

"Not as far as I'm concerned. I'll convince Abby of that too, when the time is right. I won't let her get away with splitting up the family the way she did. Now. How. Is. She?"

"She's fine," Ned said with a shrug. Then, hesitantly, he asked, "Joe, you're not planning to hurt Abby are you?"

Joe expansively held out his hands. "Hey, it's me! Would I do anything to hurt Abby? All I want is for her and me to get back together again."

"I don't want her to get hurt," Ned insisted stubbornly.

"I'm not gonna hurt her," Joe said mockingly. "You worry too much, Ned. All I want is what is mine, and I'm going to get it."

Joe's words echoed hauntingly in Ned's mind as he

drove back to Abby's place. He wondered if he should tell her that Joe was out of prison. He knew she would be upset, but still, he probably ought to warn her. He let himself in the front door and went immediately to the refrigerator to look for something to eat. Grabbing an apple, he went to the phone and dialed a number as he pulled the list Joe had given him out of his pocket to study. He frowned when he heard a busy signal at the end of the line.

Adam ran into the kitchen and flung himself into his uncle's arms. "Come on Uncle Ned!" the boy urged. "Mommy says it's time to go!"

Ned let himself be led out of the kitchen, leaving his list forgotten on the counter.

Connie watched out the window as Ned loaded Abby and Adam into his car. They were off to spend the afternoon at one of the indoor playgrounds. That should give her plenty of time to turn Abby's place upside down and shake Sloane's doubts.

She was able to do a much more thorough job than Sloane had, and certainly wasted no time admiring Abby's lingerie. It didn't take her long to find what she was looking for, laying on the counter in the kitchen by the phone.

"Here, Sloane. You think your precious Abby is innocent? Then how do you explain this!" She threw the paper on the table in front of him.

Sloane picked it up and looked at it curiously. "What is--why it's a list of all the dealers we've arrested lately, and a list of some of the ones we've been watching!"

“Exactly. And you know where I found it? Right on the counter in the kitchen. She probably stuck it there after receiving it over the phone.”

Sloane squinted at the paper. "Wonder what these numbers are? Dollar amounts? Weights?"

"Who knows," Connie said with a shrug. "Whatever, you can’t pass this off as coincidence."

Sloane's mouth formed one very thin line. He nodded. "You're right, Connie. I'm sorry."

Connie dismissed him with a careless wave. "Hey, I've been snowed before too. That's why we have partners. To keep each other in line. Now the question is what are we going to do about it?"

"I've already got an in with her. She's starting to let down her guard with me a little. I'll just keep chiseling away at her." Sloane's jaw tightened and a muscle at the corner of his mouth quivered.

Connie grinned at him. "Hey, it's good to have you back on my side."

Sloane couldn't quite manage a smile and Connie reached her hand out and touched his shoulder. "Don’t tell me she really got to you."

"No, of course not." Sloane drew himself up and managed a reassuring smile. "I'm just angry at myself for being taken, that's all."

Ned jumped at the sound of the doorbell, and then hurried to answer it. Even though he'd been expecting it, he was still startled. Abby had an evening flight, and Adam was at the baby sitter's.

"Hi Joe, L.C. Come on in."

"Hey Ned. Good to see you again," said Joe. L.C., being his usual laconic self, said nothing as he brushed by Ned and sat on the couch, immediately lighting a cigarette.

"Abby couldn't break off her drop tonight?" Asked Joe in a hurt tone.

Ned shook his head. “No. It’s a new client.”

“Did you tell her I was coming,” Joe asked.

“No. She doesn’t want anything to do with you.”

"I'm not worried. I was important to her once, and I'll be important to her again. When would be a good time to see her, Ned?"

"I don't know. I'll sound her out and get back to you." Ned reflected inwardly that Abby would be likely to throw him out on the street if he did any such thing.

"What about me?" asked L.C. He looked around for an ashtray. Finding none, he tapped his ashes out in a vase of flowers that sat on the coffee table. "I'm still waiting for my stuff," he continued. "I got clients out on the streets just dying to hand their money to me, and I ain't got nothing. When's my stock gonna be replenished?"

"Uh, I don't know," Ned said, startled by the question. He wasn't on the supply side of things. He was a dealer, like L.C.

L.C. grunted. The talk drifted to where Joe was staying, what prison was like, and the Texas Rangers' last game, a loss, as usual. Twenty minutes later Ned closed the door on Joe and L.C. with a silent sigh of relief. Not for the first time he wondered how he had ever gotten into such an awful business and how he would be able to get out of it.

"Need any more proof?" Connie raised her eyebrows challengingly.

Sloane looked grim. "I didn't need any before. All this does is make me think we got a big fish instead of a little one. And I'm ready to reel her in."

Abby softly opened the passenger door of her car

and, flipping the front seat forward, she reached into the back and gently unfastened Adam from his car seat. She could, of course, have let him stay at the sitter's till morning, but she liked having him sleep in his own bed and wake up in his own home. With the ease born of much practice, she lifted him in her arms and carried him, still asleep, to her front door. She glanced idly at the curtain on the other side of the duplex and noticed it twitch. Either Connie or Sloane was watching her come home. Abby hoped she hadn't disturbed them, but it was only 11:00 at night, and where else was she supposed to go when she came home from a flight?

Ned opened the door for her, and she carried Adam in to bed. Then she came back into the living room, her nostrils crinkling suspiciously. "Someone's been smoking ion here," she pronounced distastefully.

"Sorry, Abs. L.C. dropped by to let me know about a place going up for rent next week." Ned didn't dare mention that Joe had been in the house.

"I don't want your friends here, Ned, and I won't have people smoking in this house."

"Sorry, it won't happen again." Ned looked toward the kitchen. "You hungry? I could whip you up a sandwich or something."

"No, thanks. I'm tired. I'm going straight to bed. See

you in the morning, Ned."

Abby went into her room and decided that she really needed a shower. She let the pelting spray wash the grime off her, then pulled on a gray satin gown, enjoying the slippery feel of it against her skin. Silky lingerie was the one extravagance she permitted herself. She slept better when she felt beautiful.

Tired as she was, however, sleep refused to come. She could hear the murmur of soft voices from next door; evidently Sloane and Connie had made up after their fight. She hoped so anyway. She could almost fall for a man like Sloane. She appreciated his gentleness with Adam and admired his rugged good looks. She could almost forgive him for being a journalist, if the press had not hounded her so mercilessly when Joe had been arrested. But Sloane was married, as all the good men were.

Abby closed her eyes and tried to put Sloane Jameson out of her mind, but her dreams were sweetened by the presence of a rangy, dark-haired man with piercing blue eyes who looked suspiciously like her tenant.

CHAPTER EIGHT

The ringing of the phone cut through Sloane's dreams, waking him from a deep sleep. Groggily he raised his head from the pillow and looked around. It took him a moment to remember where he was and to realize that the phone was still ringing. Finally he put out his hand and grabbed the receiver. "H'lo," he mumbled.

"Sloane, this is Ron."

"Ron who?" Sloane asked, shaking his head in an attempt to clear it.

"Ron, Connie's husband."

"Oh. Hi Ron. I'll go get Connie." Sloane started to get out of bed.

"Connie's here with me, Sloane. She's sick."

"She's sick?"

"Yeah, some kind of flu bug has really knocked her for a loop. She can't even get out of bed. She says for you to carry on by yourself for a few days and she'll get back with you as soon as she can."

"Okay, Ron. Tell Connie not to worry. I'll be fine

here," Sloane promised. He heard Ron say good-bye and then he was left staring at an empty receiver. So poor old Connie was sick, was she? Sloane started to get up but with a groan sank back on the pillow. He didn't feel that good himself. His head was really spinning and didn't seem to be connected to his body. Maybe he'd just go back to sleep for a little while.

Abby rang Sloane's doorbell for the third time. She knew he was home because his car was parked out front. Maybe he just didn't want to be disturbed, but she did want to return his cap, which he had left in the airplane the other day. She was just about to give up and go back home when the door opened.

"Oh, hi, Sloane," Abby said brightly. "You left your cap in the airplane the other day and I wanted to return it to you." She held it out to him.

Sloane looked at the cap as if he didn't recognize it. Finally he reached out a hand. "Thanks," he croaked.

"Are you okay?" Abby knit her brow and looked at him carefully.

"Just got a bit of a bug," Sloane rubbed his hand over his forehead. As Abby looked at him, his knees buckled and he clutched the edge of the door to keep from falling.

Quickly Abby slipped her arm under his and helped him back to the bedroom where she lowered him down onto the bed.

"Sloane, you're really sick!" Her green eyes widened as they looked at him and she rested her hand against his forehead, clearly alarmed by the feverish heat.

Sloane willingly collapsed on the bed. Her hand felt deliciously cool against his flaming skin.

Abby quickly disappeared into the bathroom and reappeared with a cold wet washcloth, which she draped across his head. "Let me get you something to drink," she said. A few minutes later she was back with an ice-cold glass of apple juice. She held the glass to his lips and he took small sips that soothed his raw, aching throat.

Abby stuck a thermometer under his tongue and removed it a few moments later. She pursed her lips as she read it. "One hundred three point four." she said. "Sloane, where's Connie?"

"Connie?"

"Yes, your wife."

"Connie's not my wife, silly," Sloane said with a smile. Before he could say more, he lapsed into a feverish sleep.

Abby looked at him questioningly, wondering what he had meant by that. She laid her hand across his forehead again and chewed on her lip as she pondered what to do. She picked up the phone and called Ned next door to ask him to keep an eye on Adam. She didn't feel comfortable leaving Sloane on his own.

She wondered where Connie was. Probably at work, but did she know her husband was seriously ill? Maybe Abby should try to find Connie's work number and call the woman to come home.

On the bed, Sloane stirred restlessly and opened his eyes.

Abby bent over him. "How do you feel?"

"Mmmm," was all Sloane could manage to say.

"Sloane, where's Connie? Does she know you're sick?"

"She's with her husband," Sloane mumbled and closed his eyes again.

Abby frowned. She stood up, stretched and then went into the living room. There was a phone out there. Maybe she could find some phone numbers and get in touch with Connie.

Abby stood by the phone, hesitant to start rummaging through her tenants' desk. Then she noticed that the phone had an auto dialer. The first button was labeled "Connie." Abby picked up the receiver and pressed the auto dialer. After a few rings, an unfamiliar male voice answered the phone. “H’lo?”

“May I speak to Connie?” Abby held her breath as she waited for his reply.

“Connie’s sick and can’t come to the phone. Can I take a message?”

“No message,” Abby said quickly and put down the phone. Her heart was pounding fiercely, and she shook her head. This didn’t make any sense.

The second number on the phone’s auto dialer was labeled “work.” Making a wry face, Abby picked up the phone again and pressed the button.

A cheerful voice answered at the other end of the line. “Narcotics Investigations.”

Abby was almost too stunned to speak.

“Can I help you?” the voice repeated.

“Is Sloane Jameson there?” Abby asked nervously.

“He’s out on assignment. Who’s calling please?”

Abby hung up quickly and lowered herself into a chair in the living room. Sloane and Connie were narcs! They weren’t even married to each other! But what was their assignment? Suddenly she felt as though she’d been punched in the stomach. “They’re after Ned!” she said slowly. “It had to be. That was the only explanation.

But what should she do now? Should she tell Ned? Find an excuse to kick Sloane and Connie out of the duplex? What should she do? A slow tide of rage washed over her body. They were spying on her! They had lied to her!

Abby scowled. She would just have to wait till Sloane woke up. Then she would figure out what to do.

The next two days passed in a fitful daze for Sloane. He was dimly aware that Abby came in several times to check on him, bringing him cold glasses of juice, and hot bowls of soup which she spoon fed him. He had one moment of clarity when he remembered all the listening equipment in the other room and became fearful that Abby would somehow see it. He tried to get out of bed to go make sure the door to the room was closed, but couldn't even sit up.

At another point he remembered telling Abby that he and Connie weren't married, and wondered what he should do about that, but he simply didn't have the energy to worry about it too much.

Finally one morning he woke up from a deep sleep and for the first time in a few days, his head was clear. He swung his legs out of bed and sat at the edge for a few seconds, checking his body's response. His limbs felt weak, but the aches of the past few days were definitely gone. What's more, he actually felt hungry. As if on cue, Abby tiptoed into the room. A smile touched her lips as she saw him sitting up. "You must be feeling better," she said, planting her hands on her hips.

"I think I might just live after all," Sloane admitted ruefully. He had a vague memory of telling her that Connie wasn't his wife and wondered how he should explain that. Abby came over and put a cool hand against his forehead.

"I think your temperature's back to normal," she said. "Why don't I help you to the bathroom so you can freshen up while I get you something to eat."

It wasn't until he was actually in the bathroom, sitting gingerly on the toilet stool to shave, that Sloane realized that he was wearing just his underpants. Abby must have undressed him when she put him to bed. Despite his weakened state, the thought sent a minor thrill through him. When he came back out into the bedroom, Abby had a tray on the bed with toast and scrambled eggs, along with some juice. Sloane pulled a pair of shorts on and sat on the bed to eat. Abby leaned against the chest of drawers and looked at him speculatively.

"Now," she said. "Why don't you tell me about Connie?"

"What about Connie?" Sloane asked, shoving a forkful of eggs into his mouth.

"You had quite a lot to say while you were sick. Most of it didn't make any sense, but several times you said that

Connie wasn't your wife, that you weren't married and that she was with her husband." Abby raised her eyebrows. And I've not seen a single sign of her the past few days."

Sloane looked sad. "Connie's not here anymore," he said. "We're getting divorced. Moving into this duplex was sort of our last chance to try to get along, but it didn't work. She's moved most of her stuff out already."

"I see." Abby said noncommittally.

Sloane shrugged. "Connie's a drug addict, but she won't admit it, and she won't get help. I didn't know that when we got married, and I just can't live with her any longer."

"You did talk a lot about drugs while you were sick," Abby nodded. "You seemed very worried about something," she added.

"Oh?" Sloane said guilelessly.

"Yes, you thrashed around a lot and talked about needing proof, whatever that means." Abby lifted one shoulder in an uncertain shrug. "Are you finished?"

"What? Oh," Sloane looked down at his tray. "Yes, thanks. It was delicious."

"Well, I've got to go. I have a flight this morning. You need to take it easy, still and get as much rest as you can. I put some soda and some juice in your fridge, and there are some cans of soup on the counter. Ned will be home if you need anything and I'll check on you after I come in tonight." Abby picked up the tray and turned to leave.

"Abby?" Sloane put out a hand to stop her.

"Yes?" She paused in mid-turn and lifted a delicate eyebrow.

"Thanks. I don't know what I'd have done without you the past few days."

"Probably collapsed in the middle of the floor unable to get up, no doubt," Abby said with barely concealed laughter.

"Probably," Sloane agreed. "But I mean it. Thanks." Abby nodded and left the room with the tray. Sloane leaned back in the bed. He'd better call his supervisor and Connie and let them know the latest development, and the fact that he and Connie were no longer "married". Part of him was relieved that he would no longer need to lie to Abby about that anyway, although he would have to maintain the fiction of his and Connie's divorce. Despite himself, he liked Abby, and was even attracted to her. Lying to her was harder than anything he had ever done before, but it had to be done.

Resolutely he gave himself his daily Abby-is-a-suspected-drug-dealer talk. He put aside any problems he had reconciling the image of Abby, the drug dealer, with Abby, the bedside nurse, who had tended him through his illness, and reminded himself that he couldn't possibly be attracted to Abby. Even if she wasn't involved with drugs, she was Joe Tarleton's wife, and that alone was enough of a reason to stay away from her.

CHAPTER NINE

Abby laid back in her lawn chair, watching Adam splash in his wading pool under half-closed eyelids. The Texas sun was about to reach its zenith, and she would need to get Adam his lunch soon and put him down for his nap, but it was just so nice to lay back in the shade and let the gentle breeze play over her body as she listened to the happy noises of her son.

She had thought long and hard about what to do about her new knowledge about Sloane and finally had decided to just keep quiet about it. She was afraid if she told Ned, he would do something stupid and get himself into even more trouble. And the fact that Sloane didn't know that she knew the truth gave her a bit of an edge over him. What she couldn't admit, even to herself, was the secret feeling of satisfaction she had felt ever since she had learned that he was not married after all.

The back door slammed next door, and without looking, she cold tell by the way her hair stood on end that it was Sloane's footsteps she heard walking across the yard.

She had checked on him the night before when she came in from her flight and found that his condition was much improved. He wouldn't, he had assured her, need any more nursing. Now she opened her eyes to watch him, admiring his tall, athletic physique. He knelt down on his haunches beside Adam's pool and playfully splashed the little boy with water, groaning in mock dismay as Adam splashed back, sending sun-drenched drops of water to glisten in his dark hair and bead on his tanned forehead. He rose to a standing position with easy grace and came to add his shadow to the shade over Abby's chair. He gave her a smile that sent her pulses racing.

"Good morning!" He cast an approving glance at her tanned thighs.

Abby followed his gaze and flushed. "Good morning. I see you are feeling better," she replied, keeping her voice cool and calm.

A faint light twinkled in the depths of his eyes. "I was hoping you would agree to have lunch with me today so I could thank you for taking care of me when I was sick."

A warning voice whispered in Abby's head. She should say no. He was spying on Ned; he had lied to her.

She should stay as far away from him as possible. She opened her mouth to tell him so, but Sloane forestalled her objections with a pleading grin. "Come on. I won't take no for an answer."

As if from far away, Abby heard her voice say, "All right. That would be nice, thank you. Just let me get Adam dried off."

Sloane's mood switched abruptly from gloom and despair to happy anticipation. He clapped his hands together. "Great. Come over when you're ready."

As Abby dried her son off and dressed him, she told herself she was making a mistake. But it was only a lunch. Sloane was just being friendly, repaying an obligation. She passed by the mirror and looked approvingly at her white shorts and black-striped tank top. As an afterthought, she tied a black ribbon onto her ponytail, and then let Adam lead the way to the house next door.

Sloane whistled cheerfully as he let them in. "I've got the table all set up," he said, rubbing his hands. He brushed past her on his way to the table, carrying a glass pie plate. "Hope you like quiche."

"Did you make it?" Abby raised her eyebrows.

"No. It's from the freezer. My mother makes it in bulk and sends it to us-me, because she knows I don't cook and Connie doesn't have time. All I have to do is heat it up."

"I like it, but I'm not sure about Adam."

"Hey, I'm not stupid! It's peanut butter and jelly for him!" Sloane grabbed at the little boy and lifted him high into the air. Adam squealed delightedly. Abby's gentle laugh echoed her son's as she sat down in the seat Sloane pulled out for her.

“Zucchini quiche, spinach salad, and for dessert, fresh strawberries with whipped cream." Sloane sat down and unfolded his napkin with a flourish.

"Sounds wonderful." A smile flashed across Abby's face. Adam looked happily at his plate filled with sandwich and potato chips and proceeded to smear jelly all over his face.

Sloane watched the little boy with amusement. "Does he always eat like that?" he asked curiously.

"Of course," Abby said cheerfully. "Most three-year-olds do." She helped herself to some more quiche. "This is delicious," she said.

They ate in companionable silence for several minutes before Sloane spoke again. "Saw Ned going out bright and early this morning," he observed. "Does he have a job somewhere?"

Pain flickered across Abby's face. "No,” she said shortly.

Sloane sensed her tension and wondered if he should back off. Still, he had a job to do. “Is there a problem?” he asked.

“No,” Abby said, almost in a whisper and looked

down, trying to swallow the lump in her throat. Suddenly she wished she had not come. She was afraid- afraid of what she might say, afraid of what Sloane might learn from her.

Sloane reached his hand across the table and laid it on her arm. His fingers were warm and strong. “I can tell that you’re worried about him.”

Abby pulled away from him. Tears blinded her eyes and choked her voice. “I just remember when he was a small boy. We were such good friends then..." Her voice trailed off.

"Tell me about you and Ned," Sloane invited encouragingly. Abby dubiously lifted her eyes to his. Maybe she should talk to him about Ned. Maybe she could convince him that Ned was okay, that there was no reason to play this elaborate game he and Connie had staged. She sat back and nibbled on her quiche, trying to decide where to start.

All her memories of Ned crowded together in her mind. She sorted through them and then, at first hesitantly, the words flowed from her mouth. "We used to play in the woods all the time. It was right behind our house, the perfect playground." Abby's eyes shone at the memory. "Some developers came to tear up the woods and build a housing community. We were devastated." She swallowed hard, her eyes looking far into the past. "Ned vowed to stop them, threatened to chain himself to the bulldozer before he would let it mow down any of his beloved trees. But it didn't last long." Abby raised her brows and shook her head. "He never could hold a grudge for long. Once he realized that the new construction meant lots of nifty dirt roads perfect for bicycle riding and Cowboys and Indians, he decided that it wasn't such a bad idea after all."

Sloane exchanged a smile with her. "Did you ever fight?"

"Did we!" Abby chuckled with happy memory. "He used to play these terrible tricks. He drove all of us crazy. Once, when our parents were out, he snuck into the bathroom during my shower and stole all the towels, clothes, even my underwear. When I stepped out of the shower, streaming with water and totally naked, there was Ned, waiting for me with a camera!"

Sloane's eyes widened. "Oh no! What did you do?"

Laughter bubbled in Abby's voice. "I walked straight toward him while he blissfully snapped one photo after another. As soon as I could reach him, I grabbed the camera and smashed it against the wall." Abby demonstrated with a swing of her arm. "I can still see the look of shocked surprise on his face. I threatened to throw him through the wall unless he showed me where my clothes were."

"Did he?"

Abby snorted. "Ned wasn't stupid. I was at least a foot taller than him, so he didn't ever try to push me too far. But he also continued to play tricks on me every chance he got." She sat motionless as the memories danced through her mind. Ned had been so much fun, and now all that was changed.

God, she's good, Sloane thought for the hundredth time as he watched the play of emotions across her face. He looked in her eyes and saw something dawning there that he did not want to see, even though he knew that it was reflected in his own eyes. Quickly he jerked his hand away from her arm.

Equally flustered, Abby forced her eyes away from his face, resting her gaze for a moment on Adam. She let out a gasp when she saw the state of his hands and face, and she seized on the chance to escape the intensity of the moment. "Whoa! I'd better get him cleaned up! Can you excuse me a minute?"

"Of course, you know where the bathroom is. The washcloths are in there. I'll get the strawberries while you're gone." Sloane seemed to be just as relieved at the change of subject as she was.

Abby firmly took Adam in hand and washed his face

and hands, including behind the ear where he had somehow managed to get a streak of jelly.

Back in the kitchen, Sloane had placed a heaping bowl of strawberries at each place alongside a bowl of whipped cream. "For dipping," he explained. "That's the best way."

Abby nodded. "Of course." She sat down and dunked a strawberry into the whipped cream before taking it slowly into her mouth. "Mmm!"

Sloane's smile broadened in approval. "So, where did you fly last night?"

"San Angelo," Abby replied, licking the whipped cream off her second strawberry.

"Big drug best there. It was in the paper this morning." Sloane idly whirled a strawberry in its whipped cream and kept his voice casual.

"Really? I haven't read the paper yet. To be honest, I don't usually."

"I've been thinking of doing a story about the drug gangs. I have a lead on a big one in this area, and I think the one in San Angelo is connected to it." Sloane studied her under half closed eyelids to gauge her reaction.

"Really?" Sounds dangerous to me. Those people don't fool around."

Was that a warning, Sloane wondered. "What about

your husband's friends? Could this be the same gang he was involved in?"

Abby stood up abruptly. "I've already told you I'm not interested in you doing a story on me, and I certainly won't help you with a story about my ex-husband."

"I'm sorry, I was just asking." Sloane stood up and put his hand on her shoulder, spinning her around to look him in the eyes. "Don't go away angry."

Abby relented. "I'm not. I just don't want anything to do with what you're working on. I won't risk my son that way."

Sloane saw a chance to push her some more. "Isn't having Ned around a risk?"

"What are you talking about?" Abby demanded.

"Come on Abby. I'm not stupid. It's pretty obvious Ned is involved with some things he shouldn't be."

Abby flushed and stood in place for a few minutes, clenching and unclenching her fists as her thoughts spun out of control. "Ned is not involved with anything!" she said fiercely. Two red dots stood out angrily on her cheeks. She grabbed Adam's hand. "Thank you for lunch." She turned. "Come on, Adam. It's time to go home."

"But I haven't finished my strawberries yet!" the little boy protested.

"Too bad! Come on!"

Sloane stared after them, shaking his head. He hadn't accomplished much except for making her angry, and perhaps put the wind up her. Still, something was sure to break soon. He could feel it in his bones.

CHAPTER TEN

"Now for the next step," said Joe as he stared distractedly into space.

"Next step?" exclaimed Ned, looking up from his bologna sandwich.

“The next step in my plan to get Abby back,” replied Joe. Despite the softness of his voice and his distracted manner, there was a cold, steely look in his eyes that made Ned inwardly shiver.

Ned and Joe were sitting at the kitchen table in Joe's apartment. The centerpiece of the table was a picture of Joe and Abby on their wedding day. Joe's arm was tight around Abby's waist, his eyes gazing at her face. Even in the lifeless photo, Ned could sense the air of possessiveness-- Joe and his new acquisition.

The wall of the adjoining living room was also filled with pictures of Abby and Adam: Abby at the seat of a yellow Piper Cup, Abby lying on the grass at Trinity Park, her hair fanned out like a golden halo in the sun, Adam crawling, Adam in his bath. Abby and Adam riding a merry-go-round, and countless others. Ned recognized the pictures he had sent to Joe throughout his brother-in-law's stay in prison. He had never quite thought it was fair of Abby to cut Joe off so completely from his son, but now Ned wondered if Abby'd had the right of it after all.

Ned put his sandwich down and shifted uncomfortably in his chair. Joe had changed so much. When Ned had first met him; he had gotten in trouble twice with the FAA, once for flying too low over a nudist colony and once for using his airplane, on a dare, to herd castle through an open gate.

But while Joe had been cocky, he didn't have the hardness that he seemed to have now. Or at least he had kept it better hidden.

The hardness, the possessiveness, had not really developed until Ned had asked Joe to drop a little something off to one of Ned's acquaintances in another city. Ned hadn't meant for it to be anything more than that, a one time, small time drop. But Joe had scented the money and taken off on his own.

Joe had hounded Ned to give him the name of Ned's contacts until Ned finally gave in. Joe quickly worked his way up until he was one of the major couriers. Then he grew careless, too happy-go-lucky again, and went to prison.

Now he was out, with a hardness that had been lacking before. And he was still deeply involved with the big shots in the drug business.

“What are you going to do to Abby?” Ned asked uncomfortably.

Joe smiled slowly. “Don’t you worry about it,” he said. The corners of his mouth drew back into a malicious grin. "I am not going to hurt her. I just want to make her realize how much she needs me. By the time I am through with her, she'll come running to me for help."

Ned leaned back in his chair, his appetite for food, adventure, drugs, and high living gone, replaced by a cold knot of tension and fear. "I thought you didn't want to hurt Abby."

"I won't hurt her. Provided she comes back to me...properly, that is."

"Properly?"

"She left me, man!" snarled Joe, his anger coming to the surface and painting his face a dark red. "She left me! Divorced me, wouldn't write to me, wouldn't send pictures to me, wouldn't do anything for me! And why? Because I got caught trying to make our lives better."

Joe got up and paced furiously back and forth, hitting one wall before turning and striding towards the other one. Ned watched in fearful fascination as Joe raged on, more to himself than to the almost forgotten Ned, punctuating his remarks with fists, pointed fingers, and upswept arms.

"Now I'm gonna make her sweat! I'm gonna make her realize she needs me. That she can't just leave me to rot in jail while she raises my kid on her own. She is still mine. And after I make her beg, I'll let her come back. Provided, of course, that she wasn't the one that fingered me." Joe stopped and stroked his chin thoughtfully as this new thought worked into his brain.

"I've always wondered about that, you know? Everyone always says I just happened to be at the wrong place at the wrong time, that I had bad luck, but I wonder if I was keeping a bad woman instead. If she did finger me, I'm gonna let her hang in the wind and just take my kid instead."

Joe collapsed on the gray sofa in the living room, his black eyes glittering. "Yeah. Either way, it's gonna be fun."

Abby drew three deep breaths and forced herself to calm down. She had vowed that she wouldn't let Sloane get to her, but he had. He had opened wounds that she had thought were long healed. She had thought she had put her pain behind her a long time ago, but now, thanks to Sloane, she was reliving the pain of finding out that the man she had adored didn't care about her at all.

The memory of that night when she had found out about Joe's drug activities forced itself into her mind. It was a cool fall evening, and Joe was supposed to be on a freight run to Houston. Abby sat in a dim room in their brand new house, staring at the door, waiting for it to open, waiting for Joe to come home.

Hours crawled by. Still Abby waited. Finally Joe came in. Despite his confident air, Abby could see that he was disturbed. For a moment he didn't see her. Then his hard black eyes had met the smoldering intensity of her green ones. They stared at each other for an instant that stretched into minutes. As Abby stared, she remembered every second that had spent together. She had been immediately attracted to this dark man with the lightning mood shifts. His black, wavy hair, deep tan, and hooded black eyes were in stark contrast to his constant, hearty laughter and his carefree attitude toward life; a dark man leading a bright life.

They'd enjoyed a whirlwind romance after Ned had introduced them, flying over fireworks displays on a clear Fourth of July night, a trip to the Riverwalk in San Antonio, visiting the jazz clubs in Dallas. Their two-month courtship ended in a small wedding ceremony at her stepfather's house. Now, looking back on it all, Abby realized that through all their fun times she had never really known who Joe was. There was a secret core to the man, a darkness deeper than his eyes and not so handsome hidden beneath his light and easy manner. That night they had looked at each other in a silence that dragged on forever. Joe had been the first to look away.

"The police were here looking for you." Abby's words fell into the silence.

"Oh," said Joe casually as he tossed his jacket on the couch and moved into the bedroom. Abby followed him.

"You're wanted on suspicion of drug running. I was taken to the police station and questioned for three hours. And they searched the house." Abby forced her voice to remain calm and steady.

Joe had both his and Abby's suitcases on the bed and was throwing clothes into them. He flashed her a grin. "If they catch me, it'll be more than just a suspicion. They're chasing a friend of mine in Fort Worth. When they find out he's not me, they'll be back here real fast."

For a moment Abby was speechless. By the time she recovered her voice, he had finished packing his suitcase and was tossing her clothes into hers. Abby spoke in a soft voice that disguised the rage within her. "Joe, I'm not going with you."

Joe had not even paused. "Of course you are."

"I don't want any part of this," Abby insisted, lifting her chin determinedly.

Joe's eyes barely flickered in her direction. "Oh, you're part of it all right." There was an underlying menace in his voice.

Sheer, black fright swept through Abby. She felt her unborn child moving within her and her hand fell protectively to her stomach. "Why, Joe?" The words wrenched from her throat. "Why would you even get involved with drugs?"

Joe replied, biting the words off his tongue. "For you! And for my son! So we can have the good things in life."

"What did you do with the money?" Abby's eyes flashed scathingly. "I haven't seen any of it. Every penny we make flying freight gets spent as fast as it comes."

"Stashed it in a separate bank account. Someday we'll have enough to go away together. Live the good life." Joe slammed his suitcase closed and looked at Abby. She was shaking her head, her mouth as pale as her cheeks.

"You didn't do this for me, Joe. You did it for yourself. For the thrill of it, because it made you feel like a big shot."

Joe laughed, but his usual hearty laugh sounded menacing now. "It's time to go, Abby." He reached for her arm, and she pulled away.

"Why you-!" Joe snarled as he grasped her wrist, twisting it painfully, jerking her to him.

Forever after, Abby realized how lucky she had been that the police had come at that moment, for Joe would surely have killed her. The misery of that night still haunted her, but now, with the perspective of years, she realized that she'd never really felt love for Joe. One can't love a shell, and that was all he was.

Once he was gone, she had thrown herself into her freight business and worked on eradicating all traces of Joe from her life. Gone was her spacious home, in its place was the duplex, smaller, but all her own. When Adam was born, she knew she had everything she needed to live in contentment, and until she had met Sloane, that had been enough.

Now, for the first time since she had pushed Joe from her life, her heart swelled with a feeling she had long thought dead. Sloane's face lingered constantly around the edges of her mind, and she hungered to feel his mouth on hers. He had left a burning imprint on her that would not soon be erased. Even now, when she was angry with him, she couldn't forget his kindness and gentleness and the good times they shared when together. But she couldn’t get past the fact that he had lied to her, was still lying to her, that he was spying on her, trying to put her brother away.

"Time for your nap, Adam," she said when she was in control of her voice again. She tucked her son into bed and then settled quietly on the couch for a few moments of peace and quiet.

It was not to be, however. She heard a door slam outside and then the doorbell rang. Ned answered it and let in a man she didn’t recognize. Abby put a disapproving expression on her face. She thought she’d made it clear to Ned that she didn’t want his friends in her home

Ned forestalled Abby's protest with upraised hands. "It’s okay, Sis. This is Bob. He may have a line on a job for me at his place. I just need to change clothes. We’ll be quiet. I know Adam’s asleep.”

Abby had to admit that Bob didn't look like Ned's usual friends. He smiled at her pleasantly while Ned scrounged in his suitcase.

"Where do you work, Bob?" Abby asked curiously. She couldn't believe Ned was actually trying to get a decent job. Maybe he was finally starting to turn his life around.

"I work at a printer's. Inside sales. We have an opening in the pressroom that I think would suit Ned well."

Bob looked around the place with appreciation. "Nice duplex. You own it or rent it?"

"I own it."

"When the other side comes up for rent, would you let me know? I've been looking for a place like this. My apartment is way too small."

"I just rented it out a few days ago. A twelve-month lease."

"Oh? Well, I guess I'll have to look elsewhere."

"One of her tenants is a journalist," Ned said, coming back into the room. "His wife's a banker. They must make tons of money."

"Really? What paper does he work for?"

"I really don't know," Abby admitted. She did not tell them that Connie had moved out. Nor did she tell them that Sloane and Connie were narcotics agents.

"And you're a pilot," Bob said. "I believe you've flown some stuff for my boss. Some rush orders on occasion."

"Possibly," Abby nodded.

"These last minute orders are a pain, and the customer never understands our point of view."

"No, they don't."

"Well, I know the boss appreciates all you do for us. He says not to worry about the problem in San Angelo. We'll have some more orders for you soon." Bob stood up.

"Ready to go, Ned?"

Ned nodded and followed Bob out the door. Abby stared after them, a puzzled frown on her face. That had certainly been a weird encounter. Ned hadn't looked at all well, pale and sweaty. And what was that bit about San Angelo? The memory of Sloane talking about a big drug bust in San Angelo pricked at her mind, but how could that possibly affect a printing company? Oh well, Bob was undoubtedly schmoozing, and Ned with him.

Sloane could hardly believe his ears. He had known a break was sure to come soon. He had recognized Bob right off the bat. And that conversation had to be referring to Abby's work as a drug courier.

Last minute orders indeed! To think that he'd been feeling guilty for the way he had pushed Abby during lunch. She'd seemed so upset, but it had obviously been an act on her part. If only he wasn't so attracted to her. Dammit, why did she have to be involved with that drug ring! In another life, they could have been friends, lovers even, but now they were adversaries.

He just hadn't realized what a powerful opponent he had chosen. His mind kept turning to their shared lunch, so carefree and easy until she had left in a blaze of anger. He clung to the memory of her cool laugh rippling from her throat, her eyes sharing his enjoyment in his first small plane ride. It was impossible to believe that she was a drug dealer. It just didn't fit the image that he had been building up of her over the past several days.

Sloane clenched his jaw. Ruthlessly he created an image in his mind of Abby selling his brother the poison that had ended his life. Then he let the vision of his brother lying cold on his deathbed form in his mind. Abby was part of that horror that had killed Scott, and no matter what it took, no matter how much it wrenched his heart, he would not rest until he had enough evidence to put her behind bars.

CHAPTER ELEVEN

"So Sloane, now that we're divorced are you finding it any easier to deal with Abby?"

Sloane grimaced wryly. He and Connie were in their office at headquarters, finishing off the last of a dozen doughnuts. "She's very cautious," he said. "I keep thinking we're getting close, but I can't get her to say anything incriminating."

Connie bit into a chocolate-filled doughnut, licking the crème filling that gushed out around her painted lips. "Maybe we can really turn this divorce into an advantage."

Sloane waggled his eyebrows. "Wait, don't tell me. I'm supposed to seduce her with my rugged good looks and suave charm?" Inwardly he pushed aside the thought that he really wouldn't mind seducing Abby.

They both reached for the last doughnut. With a wave of her hand, Connie let him have it. "Well, you can," she said. "But I had in mind something different. I'm supposed to be a drug addict aren't I?"

"Yeah," Sloane said, waiting to see what she had in mind.

Connie stood up and hooked the doughnut box into a nearby trash basket. A slow smile crossed her face. "Maybe it's time I pay a little visit to Abby Tarleton."

A gleam of interest came into Sloane's eyes. "Oh?"

Connie walked toward the office door. "Go back to the duplex and listen," she directed. "When I get through with Abby Tarleton, she won't know what hit her."

Abby was comfortably ensconced on her couch, reading a book. It had been ages since she'd had time just to relax and unwind. Ned had taken Adam out for a hamburger, although by this time, thought Abby as she looked at her watch, they had probably finished their kids' meals and were on their way to the mall. There, Ned would no doubt buy Adam a couple of toys that he just couldn't live without. And, of course, they would have to stop by the video arcade to throw away five or ten dollars on the video games. She didn't really care, as long as they were out of her hair. With a little luck, she could finish her book before it was due back at the library.

She had just reached the climax of the book when

the doorbell rang. Abby looked longingly at the page in front of her. The bell rang again. With a wistful sigh, she placed a marker at her page and padded to the door, peering out the window before opening it. She started when she saw Connie outside, red eyed and sniffling.

"May I come in?" asked Connie, nervously twisting her hands together.

"Of course," said Abby, depicting an ease she certainly did not feel. "Come on in. What can I do for you?" She watched Connie warily as the other woman stepped inside.

Connie walked into the living room and stood, avoiding Abby's eyes, focusing instead on the pictures on the wall. She was impeccably dressed in a charcoal gray jacket and knee-length skirt with a white, ruffled blouse. Except for her red eyes and jittery hands, she was the perfect image of a competent businesswoman. Suddenly words exploded out of her in a rushing torrent of sound. "I shouldn't be here. You know Sloane and I have split up, don't you?" Her pert face distorted into a twisted mask of unhappiness.

Abby took a step backward. "Sloane told me," she said, holding out her hand, trying to keep her voice pleasant. Abby had always envied Connie's poise and crisply made up appearance, but now she barely recognized her. Her hair stuck out wildly from all angles on her head and hot tears rolled down her cheeks, leaving black mascara trails in their wake. Abby was just glad that Adam wasn't home. She would hate for him to be exposed to this. She lightly put a hand on Connie's shoulder. "What can I do for you?" she asked quietly.

"Oh!" Connie shook away Abby's hand and paced up and down the room, her hands gesturing wildly. "I can't even believe I'm doing this, talking to you like this! I just don't know what else to do!" Her shrill voice pierced Abby's ears.

Abby watched in fascinated horror as Connie continued to pace, first wringing her hands, then pulling at her hair. The other woman was obviously unbalanced, maybe even mentally ill. It was quite a show, she thought to herself. If she hadn't known that Connie was a narc, she would have been convinced that the other woman was deeply disturbed.

Connie stopped in midstride, as though hit by a sudden thought. With a rough laugh, she said in an almost rational voice, "What must you think of me, falling apart like this?" She sat down and laughed shrilly, touching her handkerchief to her eyes. "I just haven't had a fix in ages, and I'm about to go crazy!"

"A fix?" Abby quirked her eyebrows questioningly,

wondering what Connie was up to.

"You know--some coke." Connie laughed again. "That's why Sloane kicked me out. He's got a thing about that kind of stuff because of his brother. But Scott was just a kid; he didn't know what he was doing. I'm always careful not to overdo it. I just do enough to help me handle the pressure."

Abby felt confusion whirling up inside of her. Could Connie be telling the truth? She certainly looked like someone going through withdrawal. Maybe Abby had misinterpreted things. She shook her head. "Connie, you know better than that," she said forcefully. "Drugs don't solve anything. You need to get counseling, learn how to handle your stress. Or why don't you try jogging. That's what I always used to do when-"

Connie went on as if she hadn't heard. "My supply dried up!" She forced a sharp-edged laugh through her teeth. "Now I don't know where to go." She hesitated, measuring Abby with a sweeping gaze.

Abby's misgivings increased by the second. "Maybe you should-"

Connie's eyes lit up. "That's why I came here. You can help me! I know you can. I've heard about you!" She jumped from her seat and crossed the room to Abby's chair, looking down at Abby with a frenzied expression.

Abby tried to slow her racing pulse. "I don't know what you're talking about!" she snapped.

"I remember the stories about you in the paper," Connie said eagerly, her eyes narrowing. "Your husband was a dealer!" She seized Abby's hands. "You can help me! Tell me where I can get some stuff! I know you know!" Connie's puppy-dog eyes appealed to Abby.

Snatching her wrist away, Abby stood up. "Don't be ridiculous! I don't know what you're talking about!"

Connie clung to Abby's arm. "Of course you do! Please, Abby, you've got to help me. I've got to get a hold of some stuff, or I'll go out of my mind! I just don't know how to handle all this." Her voice started to rise again.

Abby drew herself up and turned toward the door. She'd had enough. "I really must ask you to leave." Not giving Connie a chance to protest, Abby steered her to the door. Almost before the other woman realized it, Abby had opened the door and all but pushed her onto the front step, closing the door firmly behind her.

Abby leaned against the door, relief washing over her. She didn't know what to think. Was Connie as crazy and mixed up as she had appeared? Or was she just an incredibly good actress? And if Connie and Sloane were trying to get Ned, why had Connie come to Abby.

Abby brushed her hair back from her face. She didn't

know what to believe anymore. She just knew that there was something sinister going on, and somehow she was wrapped up in the middle of it.

Connie slammed the door behind her as she entered the room she and Sloane had set up as a listening post. Sloane grinned up at her from his chair and said, "Quite a performance, Con. I'm not sure who was better, you or her."

Connie shot Sloane a furious look.

"Do you want me to buy you some jogging shoes?" Sloane continued. "I'd love to have seen your face when she said that. She really put you in your place, didn't she?" Unable to control himself any longer, Sloane threw back his head and howled with laughter.

Connie's glare dissolved into a rueful look. "She didn't exactly rise to the bait, did she?" She collapsed in the chair across from him.

"It almost makes you wonder if she is innocent and we're on the wrong track," said Sloane, throwing the idea out once more to test her reaction.

Now it was Connie's turn to howl. "Sloane," she said patiently. "I know you've fallen for her, and she does seem like a nice person, but there's too much evidence linking her to this drug operation." She counted on her fingers as she reeled off the list. "There's Joe's letters from prison, the stuff we found in her duplex, the meeting we overheard between Joe, Ned, and L.C., those phone calls, the pay off you witnessed and everything else."

Sloane nodded gloomily. Catching Connie's discerning eye, he brightened his expression. "No, you're right. She's just a very smart, very cautious lady. But we'll break her. Just be patient. We'll break her."

"I wonder..." Connie's face blanked for a moment as she followed a new line of thought. "You don't think that she could be on to us, do you?"

Sloane considered the idea. Perhaps he had said more than he'd realized when he was sick. He rejected the thought. "No, I think she's just cautious." Even as he spoke, however, his heart was screaming in protest. Sloane resolutely ran through the litany of evidence against Abby, reminding himself that she was Joe Tarleton's wife and ending, as he always did, with the vision of his brother lying dead on the bed. Connie was right, as usual. This was one time when his head would have to triumph over his heart.

Abby placed her hands on the small of her back and stretched as she tucked Adam, already half asleep, into bed.

He had come home from his outing with Ned with a new toy from McDonald's and some prizes he'd won at the video arcade. He clutched one of the toys, a toy car, in one chubby fist as he drifted off to sleep. Abby bestowed one last smile on him and then tiptoed out of the room, closing the door gently.

In the living room Ned was sprawled on the couch, watching TV and eating popcorn. Abby looked at the screen; he was watching some cops and robbers show. She didn't think she could get into it. "I think I'll go out for a walk, Ned," she said.

Ned waved at her as she went out the door. Abby stepped outside into the still warm night air. She turned toward the street, planning to walk up around the high school but at the end of her walk, she turned and somehow ended up at Sloane's doorstep. She wasn't quite sure why she was there, she just felt after her visit from Connie that she needed to talk to him.

Sloane lifted an eyebrow in surprise when he opened the door and saw her there. He was wearing cut-off jeans and nothing else.

Abby blushed as her eyes roamed up his muscled chest before stopping at his face.

"Is anything wrong?" Sloane asked concernedly.

"Oh no," Abby said quickly. "Did I catch you at a bad

time?"

"No, not at all." Sloane moved away from the door. "Come on in."

Abby followed him inside and stopped just inside the door, suddenly unsure of what to do. Sloane casually crossed the room and sat down on his couch, grinning up at her. "Come on. Have a seat," he invited. "Can I get you something?"

"No," Abby said hastily. "I just wanted to talk to you." She perched gingerly on the edge of the large easy chair and rested her hands on her knees. "Connie came to see me today." As she spoke, she wondered what had made her come to Sloane. Somehow, she hoped that she could find out what, exactly was going on.

"Oh?" Sloane's expression suddenly became guarded.

Abby bit her lip nervously. "She was very- agitated. She seemed to think I could help her get some drugs. I had to ask her to leave, practically throw her out of my house."

"I'm sorry," Sloane said. "Why would she come to you like that?"

Abby heaved a sigh. "She'd heard about my ex-husband," she said in a soft voice. She lowered her head, her eyes suddenly brimming with tears.

Sloane's eyes studied her intently. "Does that happen

often?" he asked.

"Not until recently," Abby said, shaking her head vigorously. "Oh, after he was first arrested there were a bunch of crackpot calls, but once I moved here and got an unlisted number, that dropped off. But lately such weird things have been happening-" She paused and bit her lip again. "Just when I'd begun to think I was finally free of him. Now I don't think I can ever get away from him."

"Have you heard from him?"

"No!" Abby said quickly. "It's just-" She stopped herself and stood up. "I'm sorry," she said. "You've got enough problems right now. I certainly didn't mean to dump mine on you. I just wanted to tell you about Connie." She quickly turned away but like a flash, Sloane was between her and the door, blocking her path.

"I'm sorry she upset you," he said in a low voice that sent tremors through her body.

"It's okay. It's not your fault," Abby said quickly. "I'm sorry. I shouldn't have come here."

"Yes you should," Sloane said, looking at her with eyes that were suddenly deep and compelling.

Abby took a step backward. Looking at the base of her neck, Sloane could see the flutter of her pulse. He put out a hand and laid it on her bare shoulder. Her skin was so soft, so smooth. "You're upset," he said, stroking her shoulder lightly. "Come on, sit down." Taking her arm he led her back to the couch. "Tell me what's going on."

In a daze, Abby sat down. Sloane settled beside her and looked at her expectantly. He didn't let go of her. Abby looked down for a moment at their joined hands, their fingers clasped gently, her hand trembling slightly at his touch. “Sloane, when you were sick, you said some things-“ she paused.

“What did I say?” Sloane held his breath.

“You said several times that Connie wasn’t your wife.”

“Because we’re getting a divorce,” Sloane said firmly. “I’m upset about it.”

“Yes, but-“ suddenly Abby was afraid to tell him what she thought. She took a deep breath and then said, “You were so sick, I was worried about you. So I used the auto dialer on your phone to try to call Connie.”

Sloane felt a sinking sensation inside his chest. How stupid could he have been?

“When I called, a man answered and said she couldn’t come to the phone because she was sick.”

“So what is your point?” Sloane asked pointedly. “Connie and I had a fight and she went back to her parents’ house. I’ve had that phone since before she and I were married.”

"But then I dialed the other number. The one that is labeled 'work'."

Sloane frowned. "And?"

"I reached the narcotics office. I asked for you and they said you were on assignment."

"I work for a newspaper Abby," Sloane said patiently. "I'm usually out on assignment."

"But why did the woman say that it was the narcotics investigations when she answered the phone?"

"Are you sure she said 'Narcotics Investigations'? We usually answer the phone with 'Newspaper Investigation.'"

Abby bit her lip, still confused. "I might have misunderstood," she said with a frown.

"Is that what this is about?" Sloane said. "You think I'm a narc?"

"I know that Ned's involved in something that I'd just as soon not know about," Abby said in a very low voice. "And I thought you and Connie were spying on us to get to Ned. But then today, when Connie came by, I didn't know what to think. I-"

Sloane grabbed her hands and looked into her eyes with a fierce intensity. "Abby-" he stopped and realized he didn't know what to say. He was tired of this game he was playing, tired of lying to Abby, tired of fighting his own feelings for her.

“It’s all just like a nightmare,” Abby continued as though she hadn’t heard him. “It’s bringing everything with Joe back again. I didn’t know who to trust then. The police were watching me, the press was hounding me, and I found out my husband was not who I thought he was.”

"How did you feel when you found out about Joe?" Sloane prompted.

"Angry. Hurt. Betrayed." Abby spoke mechanically and closed her eyes, remembering the pain. "I thought we were so happy but suddenly my entire world came crashing down. My husband was arrested. My parents died. And I lost just about everything I had. For the first time in my life I had to worry about money, worry about where my next meal was coming from. And when Adam came-" A tear squeezed out from under her eyelid and trickled down her cheek. "When Adam came I had to worry about him. It wouldn't have been so bad if I'd been by myself. I can take care of myself," Abby repeated with emphasis. "But I had to look after Adam too. I don't think I'll ever forgive Joe. Never!" She repeated the words with a fierceness that caught Sloane by surprise.

"Had you no idea that Joe was dealing drugs?"

"None. I should have, I guess. There were signs. But I just couldn't believe he'd do that. I didn't want to believe it, I guess. When the police came, the night they arrested him, it was a complete and total shock."

Sloane rubbed his thumb slowly over her palm. Looking in her eyes, he somehow knew that she was telling the truth. His heart had been telling him almost since the beginning that Abby could not be involved in anything illegal, and now, sitting beside her and looking at the pain on her face, Sloane knew that his heart must be right. He squeezed her hand.

“I don’t want to go through that again, Sloane,” Abby said, wiping away a tear. “I thought I could trust you, but now, I don’t know what’s going on or who you are.”

Sloane sighed. “I don’t blame you for being confused,” he said. “I know what it’s like to find out that someone you love is a complete stranger.” The memory of his brother came, unbidden, to the forefront of his mind.

Abby raised her head and looked at him. His words hit her right in the heart. She wanted to trust him; she had to trust somebody. She must have been mistaken about him and Connie being narcs. He was obviously broken up about his wife. "How long have you known about Connie?" she asked.

"What? Oh-" Sloane was caught off guard by her question. Quickly he reminded himself that he was playing a role, one that was becoming increasingly hard to play. "Almost since we've been married," he said quickly, absent-mindedly. He didn't want to talk about Connie right now. He wanted to look into Abby's eyes, to lose himself in those green depths.

"I don't suppose she'd consider counseling?"

"No," Sloane said, his voice dropping an octave. His thumb moved from her palm and started massaging her wrist, his light, feather-like strokes dancing like electricity upon her skin. "Abby," he said softly in a strangled voice.

"Yes."

"I want to kiss you." Without waiting for her reply, Sloane dropped his lips to hers and, at first hesitantly, then as he felt her slow response, he covered her mouth with his and drew her to him. His tongue pried apart her lips and found her tongue, intertwining deliciously. Her mouth was soft and warm against his, and he put his arms around her and pulled her to him, feeling her breasts beneath her thin shirt crushed up against him. "I've wanted to do this ever since I met you," Sloane murmured before his lips again took possession of hers.

Abby felt her head ringing, felt the hairs on his chest brushing against her shirt. His hands rubbed warm circles on her back, moving down to the bottom of her shirt and coming up from underneath. She gasped at the feel of his fingers on her bare back. Her hands moved up to his head and buried them in his hair, twisting it about her fingers.

Sloane's mouth moved down her chin, leaving a trail of soft kisses as he worked his way down her neck to the hollow at the base of her throat. He pulled one strap of her tank shirt off her shoulder and kissed her there. Then he went to the other side. He tugged at her shirt. "May I?" he asked.

Abby took a deep breath. She'd not made love to anybody since Joe had been arrested, and knew that she shouldn't be doing this with Sloane now, but she couldn't stop herself. She nodded and Sloane pulled her shirt off. A smile crossed his face as he looked at her pert breasts beneath her thin bra. Her nipples hardened and he touched one gently with his finger. Unconsciously, Abby thrust herself out to meet him and he laughed, rubbing his finger teasingly against the silky fabric of her bra. With a quick motion he reached behind her and unfastened it, and she was bared to him.

For a moment he just looked from one breast to the other, then with a guttural moan he lowered his head and lavished kisses on her breasts, her nipples, swirling each one with his tongue. Abby moaned with pleasure and pressed against him. He clasped her to him and she rubbed herself against him, relishing the friction of his hairy chest against her sensitive nipples.

"You are so lovely," Sloane said in a throaty voice.

Abby smiled to hear it. She'd never thought of herself as pretty but now, in his arms, she felt beautiful. Her hands trilled lightly over his back, exploring the corded muscles there. Holding the back of her head, Sloane laid her out on the couch and stretched his body out on top of hers. Abby let out a gasp of surprise as she felt his arousal pressing against her stomach. Sloane smiled at her and she reached up to brush the hair out of his eyes, just as she had so often dreamed of doing.

Sloane looked down at her lying beneath him. His body was trembling with the effort of holding himself back. He wanted to tear her clothes off and plunge himself into her but knew he had to take it slow and easy. He didn't want to scare her, didn't want to hurt her.

She felt so fragile but her eyes were smoky with desire and her hands dropped tentatively to his shorts, exploring along the waistband. Sloane shuddered. He couldn't hold back much longer. He covered her mouth again, caressing her tongue with his, then raised himself off her long enough to tug at the zipper of her shorts. Inch by agonizing inch he pulled it down and Abby squirmed as she felt his fingers moving down along the front of her panties. At last the zipper was undone and she raised her hips as he pulled her shorts and panties off at once.

"Your turn," Abby said and grasped the zipper of his

pants. Sloane let out a moan as she unzipped his pants and then they were both naked. Abby's eyes widened as he stood revealed before her. Sloane's eyes looked down at her, staring at her face, flushed with desire, moving down to her breasts, taut with urgency, and on down to the bright thatch at the top of her legs. Abby parted her thighs at his look and gave a little whimper. What was he waiting for?

Sloane was having a hard time holding himself back. He took several deep breaths and forced himself to stand still and look at her, to try to regain some control. Finally he lowered himself on top of her and lay, naked, against her.

Again, he held still, unmoving. Abby pressed herself against him, thrusting upward and suddenly, with a loud groan, Sloane moved to enter her, pushing till he was enveloped in her warm, satiny depths. Again he waited till her felt her contracting around him and then he started to move, at first slowly, and then faster as he lost all semblance of control. Abby felt each thrust take him deeper inside her and she surged upward to meet him. They both cried out till she couldn't tell which voice was his and which hers as the night exploded into a thousand stars around them and he collapsed, spent, on top of her.

They both lay there, reluctant to move. Sloane covered her face with kisses and finally pushed himself off of her. He looked down at her, her eyes half closed, her cheeks rosy. Suddenly it struck him what he had done. He had just made love to Joe Tarleton's wife. Now, what had only a moment before seemed so right, now seemed to be a betrayal of his brother and all the other people everywhere killed by drugs. He looked at her, no longer seeing the desirable woman of a few moments ago, seeing only the drug dealer's wife. His face grimaced with revulsion and he quickly stood up.

Abby caught the wisp of a look that crossed his face. "What's wrong, Sloane?" she asked in a voice still thick with lovemaking.

"Nothing," Sloane said shortly. He reached for his shorts and pulled them on.

Abby sat up and propped herself up on one elbow. Sloane scrabbled through the clothes on the floor and handed hers to her. Confused, Abby dressed herself. When finished, she stood up and reached a hand out to touch him on the shoulder. "Are you sorry?" she asked, almost not wanting to know the answer.

Sloane stiffened. He started to answer in the affirmative, but caught himself. He wasn't sorry. He had wanted to make love to Abby, and what's more, he wanted to do it again. He wouldn't, of course, he wouldn't let himself lose control like that again, but he couldn't be sorry he had done it. He had never experienced anything like it before and doubted he ever would again. "No," he said in a deflated voice. "No. I'm not sorry."

"Neither am l." Abby waited for a reply, but he stood impassive. Her hand dropped by her side and she turned to quietly let herself out the door. "Good bye Sloane," she whispered, and then quickly slipped out the door.

Sloane moved to the window and, lifting the edge of the curtain, watched as she stumbled over to her own side of the duplex. He sighed. Tomorrow he would call his supervisor and tell her that he was wasting his time. Abby Tarleton may be a lot of things, but she was not involved with her ex-husband's drug ring. It was time for him to move on, and the sooner the better. He needed to move on to another assignment and put Joe Tarleton's wife out of his mind and out of his life.

CHAPTER TWELVE

Sloane was not able to contact his supervisor the next day as she was out of the office. He didn't feel that closing down the stakeout was of great enough importance to track her down on a well earned day off, so he stayed inside the duplex, afraid he might run into Abby outside. Idly he kept an ear on the conversations next door, but they were quite normal. Ned watched TV all day and Abby was on a flight. No one said anything about drugs.

He did try to call Connie at her home, but her husband said he hadn't seen her since she had left to meet Sloane at headquarters the day before. Sloane was slightly surprised that Connie would go off on her own without leaving word with someone, but he wasn't too concerned.

The next day, however, Ron reported that he still had not heard from Connie. Sloane called his supervisor and learned that she had not heard from Connie either. "I'll notify all the field agents that she's out there somewhere, Sloane. You hold things down at your end."

Sloane chewed his lip thoughtfully. He had been

going to tell his supervisor that he wanted to shut down the stakeout, but now he wasn't so sure. Could Connie's disappearance have anything to do with her visit to Abby? Maybe Connie was right and he was wrong about Abby. Maybe she was involved in the drug ring after all. He mentioned his suspicions to his supervisor and added, "I'm thinking it may be time to apply some more pressure at this end."

“Such as?"

"Give Connie till late this afternoon to get some word to us. If we haven't heard from her by then, how about arresting Ned?"

"All right. I'll arrange it. Keep in touch, Sloane."

Sloane stared at the phone for a second, willing it to ring, but it defiantly remained silent. A chill dread spread through his body. Their cover must have been blown. Somehow Abby had discovered who they really were and had moved to eliminate Connie from the picture, either for revenge or to keep her from finding out anything more. Had Abby made her move before or after her visit to him, he wondered. Maybe her visit had just been her way of keeping him distracted so that her people could take care of Connie.

On a whim, Sloane went next door. After several minutes, Abby opened the door clad in a navy blue bathrobe. Her usually lively eyes were worn with weariness and her hair was disheveled, a golden aura circling her head.

"I'm sorry, I didn't mean to wake you up." Sloane's eye was caught by a lacy frill peeping from the v-neck of her robe, and in spite of himself, he felt a thrill as he remembered their lovemaking only a few short days ago.

"What's the matter, Sloane?" Abby's voice was still thick with sleep, and she raised her eyebrows in a futile attempt to become more alert.

"Have you seen Connie?" There was an edge to his voice.

"Connie?" she said, clearly surprised that he had asked her. "No, not lately. I've been gone since yesterday morning. Had a long flight, didn't get in till a couple of hours ago."

"Where to?" Sloane barked. A cold knot formed in his stomach. Abby's wide-eyed innocence didn't fool him one bit. What had her cargo been? Had Connie been bundled aboard that plane?

Abby moved out of the doorway, puzzled by his attitude. "El Paso." She drew her breath in sharply as his eyes flashed imperiously. "Sloane, what's wrong. You look upset. Maybe you'd better come in and I'll get us some coffee."

El Paso? Sloane's thoughts swarmed dangerously in his head. That was much too close to the border for his peace of mind. If Connie had been on that plane, she might already have been smuggled over the border into Mexico. He followed Abby into the living room, practically tripping over her heels. His head swiveled as he looked around suspiciously. "Where's Ned?"

Abby turned on her way to the kitchen. "He got a job. At a printer's. I'm hoping he's maybe going to settle down at last."

Sloane shut out the hope in her voice. "Which printer's?"

"I don't know--oh, wait, yes I do because I've flown freight for them." Abby's voice from the kitchen was muffled. "It's Print Fast, over in the industrial part of town." She re-entered the room carrying two steaming mugs of coffee. "Now sit down, and tell me what's wrong." She curled herself up in a corner of the couch and peered at him over the edge of her cup.

Sloane reluctantly lowered himself to a chair. The neck of her robe had fallen further open, offering a glimpse of the curve of a creamy white breast against a green satin gown. Sloane took a deep breath and forced himself to remain calm. If he was going to help Connie, he had to keep control of the situation. "She's disappeared," he said, passing his hand over his eyes. "She's been staying with a friend since we split up, and her friend says she hasn't been home since she came over to your house the other night. No one has seen her."

His words struck straight at Abby's heart. Her hand flew to her mouth. Oh, why hadn't she seen this coming? Connie had been so upset when she had come to visit her, and she, Abby, had just brushed her off. "Oh Sloane!" Abby said softly. "She was awfully upset when she left here. She seemed desperate to find some drugs."

Sloane hesitated, realizing he had not thought this out carefully enough. Was he ready to break cover, confront Abby with his knowledge? Or should he continue to play the part of the aggrieved husband? The drug agent part of him was all for forging ahead and dragging the truth out of Abby, but another part of him held back. He just couldn't be sure, not yet anyway. And if Abby did not know anything about Connie's disappearance, breaking his cover could be a grave mistake.

He shook his head decisively. "I'm worried about her. Just because we've split up doesn't mean I'm not concerned anymore." Unconsciously he settled into the role of the puzzled husband. "You're a woman," he said. "Where would she go?"

Abby cast her mind back. "I went home. To my parents," she said softly. "Have you checked with her mom and dad?"

Sloane shook his head. Inside, he felt torn in two. He knew that Abby had to be deeply involved with the drug ring, and if she knew anything about Connie's disappearance, then everything she was saying now was just a clever charade. Could she possibly be playing with him, like a cat with a wounded bird? Sloane felt a cold shiver ripple down his spine. It was hard to believe that this seemingly pleasant woman, the loving mother of a young child, could be so cruel. His mind was aswim in a haze of feelings and logic, but his heart refused to believe what his mind told him. He faltered, and then with an iron will, got a grip on himself. If Connie was still alive, she would be depending on his clear thinking to get her out of whatever mess she was in.

"Have you checked the bank to see if she's at work? Connie's very responsible, you know. I'm sure she wouldn't just dump her job," Abby suggested.

"No. I didn't think of that. I've just been out of my mind." Sloane reached for his coffee cup and with trembling hands lifted it to his lips. Somehow, his hand slipped and the cup dropped, spilling coffee all over himself and his chair. Instantly Abby was on her feet, wiping him with a handkerchief. "I'm sorry. I spilled coffee all over your chair," Sloane said.

"It's okay," Abby replied as she mopped the front of his shirt. "Let me go get a towel. Why don't you go to the bathroom and clean yourself off? Did you get burned? The coffee was awfully hot! Here, let's take a look." Quickly she unbuttoned his shirt, inhaling slightly as she saw the red burn mark on his chest. "Here, let's go get some cold water on this. It's the best thing, you know." Taking him firmly by the hand, as though he were no older than Adam, she led him into the bathroom and, running a washcloth under the cold water, pressed it lightly against the burn on his chest.

Sloane looked down at her blonde head. He inhaled slightly and caught the faint whiff of her perfume. Her fingers light on his chest sent thrills through his body, and it was with great effort that he kept from pulling her into his arms. Firmly he reminded himself that this woman had in all probability engineered the disappearance of his partner.

"There," Abby looked up finally. "Is that better?" Her robe had come all the way open, baring for his gaze her body enveloped in a sheer, shimmering jade gown which matched the green of her eyes.

"Yes, thank you," Sloane said thickly. Their bodies were so close that he could feel the heat emanating from her and his mind turned involuntarily to their lovemaking of the other night.

Abby's eyes dropped down his front to his jeans, where some of the coffee had landed in his lap. "Did you burn-" An unwelcome blush crept into her cheeks.

"What would you do if I did?" Sloane asked. His silky voice held a challenge.

Abby turned away suddenly. Without warning, Sloane caught her shoulders and turned her back almost roughly. Putting his finger under her chin, he forced her eyes up to meet his. "Where is Connie?" he demanded through clenched teeth.

"What do you mean?" Abby stammered.

He could almost hear her heart beating. Could see the sudden flicker of fear in her eyes. Yes, he thought. She does know. His mind burned with the memory of Connie. How she had taken a young rookie cop under her wing and shown him the ropes, how she had made him part of her family, inviting him to frequent dinners with her and her husband, how she had pushed him out of the way of a speeding car that had hit her instead. She had nearly died then, to save his life.

The thought that this scheming drug dealer with her innocent act might have done something to hurt Connie inflamed him. The passion he felt for Abby was transformed and added to the fuel of his anger. Uncertainty vanished for the moment as his only thought was how to break this woman. "It's your fault!" he repeated.

"No!" The thought tore at Abby's insides. Had Connie somehow learned what she and Sloane had done, she wondered. Was that why she had left?"

"Don't bother denying it." Sloane bent his face to hers till he felt her breath hot on his lips. Abby tried to back away but he held her tightly in his grasp.

"Sloane, don't!" Abby felt as though her breath were cut off. Her pulse beat erratically at the threatening note in his deep voice.

"Where is she?" he demanded.

"I don't know!" Abby wrenched herself away from him with a choking cry.

Sloane's anger became a scalding fury, and he didn't care whether he hurt her or not. It felt good to bury his confusion and doubt in his anger. It was what he should have been doing all along, instead of getting caught up in the web of deceit Abby had woven. He couldn't deny the evidence any longer. Abby was guilty. "I'll make you tell me, Abby! You can't resist me forever!"

Abby remained absolutely motionless for a moment. She inhaled deeply, trying to push the rage out of her body. Relentlessly, Sloane continued, his words hammering at her ears. "Where is she?" He towered over her, his face tight and menacing.

Determinedly, Abby mustered her strength and pushed him away. She glared at him furiously. "I think you'd better leave."

"Oh no, you don't" Sloane drawled. He moved toward her and she backed away till she came up against the wall and couldn't go any further.

"This won't help you get Connie back!" she warned.

Sloane stopped and looked at her warily. "What will?"

Abby drew her tongue across he lips. "Go home and call everyone she knows. Someone is bound to have heard from her. Barring that, wait by the phone. Surely you will hear something soon."

Sloane shot her a withering stare. "All right. But if I don't hear something soon," he reached out and pressed his finger warningly against her cheek. "I'll be back."

Abby slumped against the wall until she heard the door slam.

Then she dragged herself to her bed and crawled wearily in, trying to calm the rapid beating of her heart.

He's upset, she tried to tell herself. Normally he wouldn't have done that. But a stab of guilt lay buried in her breast, a feeling that she was indeed responsible for Connie's leaving. She had looked lustfully at Sloane and fantasized about him ever since he had moved in. She had even made love to him. Glorious, rapturous love. No wonder Sloane had acted so strangely when they were finished the other night. He must have been wracked with guilt over making love to her. It was obvious he was still in love with Connie. She should have realized that he was just as off limits to her as he had been before the breakup of his marriage.

Furious at her vulnerability to him, Abby yielded to the compulsive sobs that engulfed her as she clutched the blankets to her chest, pummeling her pillow in an attempt to drive them out of her body.

Sloane listened to her sobs emanating from the listening equipment set up in his room. Part of him wanted to run next door and hold her, to kiss away her tears and make up for the rough treatment she had endured at his hands. But the sure knowledge that Abby held the key to Connie's disappearance held him back. She had said he would hear about Connie soon. He had to hold on to that. Abby might seem like a confused and desirable young woman. But he knew now that she was a devious and dangerous criminal.

CHAPTER THIRTEEN

Sloane watched from, the window as Abby carried Adam into the house, followed by Ned. Quickly he went to the phone and called his supervisor. "Has anyone heard from Connie yet?" he asked.

"No. Have you any word at your end?"

"No. I think it's time to apply more pressure. She and Ned are home now. Get someone over here and arrest Ned. And, let's not be in too big a hurry to let him out on bail."

"Gotcha."

Sloane watched with satisfaction as the police car pulled up in front of the duplex several minutes later. He heard the doorbell ring and listened intently at his station in the bedroom.

Abby answered the door. She stared blankly at the uniformed police officers outside. "Yes?"

"We're looking for Ned Harris."

Abby's mouth opened in dismay. She turned. "Ned? There are some policemen here for you." This scene was sickeningly familiar. What had Ned done now, she wondered.

"Ned Harris?" the younger policeman asked as Ned came into view.

"Yeah?" Ned sounded nervous.

"We have a warrant for your arrest."

"On what charges?" Abby asked angrily.

"We have evidence that he's been selling drugs, Ma-am."

"But-" Abby started to protest, but Ned hushed her with a look.

"It's okay, Abs." He scrounged in his pocket and pulled out a small address book. "Give my boss a call for me, will ya? Let him know what's happened. And follow me down to the station and bail me out. You know the routine."

Abby bit her lip as she watched the police lead Ned to the patrol car. Then she hurried to the phone, but instead of phoning Ned's boss, she called her lawyer, the one who had helped her through the hard times when Joe had been arrested. "Mr. Hestler, this is Abby Tarleton. My brother Ned has just been arrested on charges of drug dealing."

"Has he? I'm sorry to hear that, Mrs. Tarleton. Do you want me to meet you at the station?"

"Yes, please." Abby hung up the phone and gave her sitter a quick call to see if she could drop Adam off at her house. Then she woke Adam from his nap and carried him to the car.

Several minutes later she looked at Ned across a broad, metal table. They were in a worn, bare room with white walls, old, faded brown tiles, three wooden chairs, the table, and nothing else. "I think you had better tell me about it, Ned. How deep are you in?" asked Abby without any preliminary chitchat. Her eyes blazed green fire. How dare he put her through this again?

"Not very, Abs," said Ned, avoiding her eyes. "I've bought a little and sold a little, but not much else. Small stuff, really."

Abby's eyes darkened dangerously. "You're lying. You're holding out on me little brother, and you better stop it right now."

Ned hunched over the table and sighed in resignation, looking at a spot on the floor where the tile had broken off, showing the concrete beneath. "Abs, watch yourself. You're in danger!"

Abby tried to comprehend what Ned had said. "What are you talking about?" Her voice was cold and hard.

"You're being set up. You need to get to Sloane."

"Sloane? What's he got to do with this?" Abby said in a tone of flat disbelief.

"Yeah. He's a narc. Both of them are. They busted a

friend of mine last year. They're watching your place, Abs. They're watching you, hoping you'll lead them to the other people in the gang."

Again Abby was momentarily shocked into speechlessness. This time, though, she couldn't form any coherent thoughts. Instead, pure emotion flickered through her soul. Startled hurt turned into white, hot anger. "Why do they think that?" she demanded. Her nostrils flared. She had been right about Sloane and Connie! Sloane had lied to her. Only from what Ned was saying, they weren’t after him, but were trying to get something on her! To think she had let Sloane make love to her, that she had taken pleasure in his arms!

Ned squirmed, eyes still on the floor. "I don't know, Abs, except maybe the fact that you used to be married to Joe and that you're always looking out for me." He lifted his shoulder in a helpless shrug. "Maybe they figure that a pilot flying freight is a great cover for carrying drugs. It was for Joe."

Abby abruptly stood up. She wanted to run around and scream, get some physical release from the tension and anger she felt. She placed her hands on her hips and stretched, looking up at the water-splattered ceiling. "They're crazy! They're absolutely crazy!" Suddenly she rounded on Ned like a wolf pouncing on a sheep. "And what have you told them, little brother?"

Ned finished. "Nothing but the truth, Abs. I swear it. I came clean on what I've been doing, which means that you won't have to worry about me being a house guest any longer." Ned's half-hearted attempt at levity fell flat. "Honest, Abs! I told them the truth. I told them you don't and never did have anything to do with drugs, and that you were only taking care of me out of some misguided sense of family loyalty."

At the misery in Ned's voice, Abby's gaze softened. She took a deep breath and said, "Okay, Ned. I believe you. I only hope the police do too." Her hand dropped to his shoulder. "Mr. Hestler is coming to arrange your bail. We'll get you out of here."

"Thanks, Abs. I knew I could count on you," Ned said as she left the room.

Sloane raised his eyebrows when he heard the ring of the doorbell. Could she be ready to make a deal? He waited until she rung a second time before he opened the door. "Yes?"

Without waiting to be asked, Abby pushed her way inside. She glared at him with burning, reproachful eyes.

"Ned tells me you're a narc!"

Sloane lifted an eyebrow. "A narc?"

His tone aroused and infuriated her. "Oh, don't play innocent with me! All this time you've been lying to me, spying on me and my family!" Abby felt her hands clenching at her sides.

"I'm not the only one who's been lying, Abby," Sloane said dangerously. His jaw tightened. "Connie is still missing, you know."

"She's not even your wife!" Abby spat.

"No, she's my partner, as you well know. And I want to know what you did with her." His voice was cold and lashing as his eyes blazed down into hers.

"What I-" Abby broke off and rubbed her temples with her fists. She couldn't believe what she was hearing. "You can't think I had anything to do with this. If you've been spying on me, then you know I don't have anything to do with drugs!"

Sloane rocked back on his heels and folded his arms, regarding her through half lowered eyelids. "Oh, you're good, Abby Tarleton. But not good enough. I have plenty on you right now. The only reason you're not in jail along with your brother is because of Connie. I'll make a deal with you. Give me Connie, safe and sound, and I'll talk to the D.A. You could be out in a year, maybe less. Maybe even a suspended sentence."

Abby shot him a withering look. "You would make a bargain with someone you suspected of dealing in drugs. What kind of monster are you?"

Her reaction was not what Sloane had expected. He rocked back on his heels, and his blue eyes studied her speculatively. What was her game now?

Abby threw back her head and placed her hands on her hips. "If I am a drug dealer, I deserve to be behind bars for the rest of my life."

Her reaction seemed to amuse him. "Is this a confession?"

Abby couldn't fail to catch the note of sarcasm in his voice. She raised her chin with a cool stare in his direction. "The only things I'm guilty of are marrying a louse and being a good sister. Whatever evidence you have must be faked." She emphasized her words with a haughty sniff.

Sloane caught her wrist in an iron grasp. "I don't fake evidence." His voice was as cold as tempered steel.

Abby met his accusing eyes without flinching. "Someone did," she said with easy defiance, tossing her head and pulling her hand away from him.

"I want Connie back, Abby," Sloane said with deceptive calm. "She has a husband waiting for her. Think of him." He appealed to her with his eyes.

Abby's eyes flashed with emerald fire. She chose her words carefully, speaking slowly and distinctly to make sure he understood. "Get this straight. I don't have any idea where Connie is. You're wasting your time watching me. Furthermore," Abby drew herself up. "I'll be talking to my lawyer tomorrow about drawing up eviction papers. You'd better start packing tonight." Abby pivoted on her heel and strode to the door, but Sloane caught her arm and yanked her back to him.

"Oh no, Abby," he said in a voice that matched the cold glint in his eyes. "You're not walking out on me. I'm not letting you leave till you tell me where Connie is."

Abby shot him a furious look. "Then I guess I'll be here a long time because I don't know where she is!"

Sloane leaned back against the wall, his mouth spread into a thin-lipped smile. "Oh, I can wait. I have nothing better to do," he said blandly.

Abby felt her flesh color. She clenched her teeth in fury as Sloane moved closer, looking down at her intensely. Suddenly, before she could protest, he roughly covered her mouth with his, brutally thrusting his tongue inside, moving one hand down her back and forcing her upward into his arms. Gone was the tenderness he had shown her the other night, replaced by a hard, urgent, angry need.

With an abrupt shove, Abby pushed him away from

her. She raised her chin defiantly and looked at him with a steely glint in her eye. "Don't you ever touch me again," she warned in an icy voice. She whirled toward the door, her hair flying behind her.

"Where do you think you're going?" Sloane demanded.

Abby struggled to keep her fragile self-control. "I'm going home," she said frigidly. "For the last time, I don't know where your precious Connie is. I am not involved with drugs. And I never want to see you again." With solid dignity she walked to the door, leaving him alone with his anger.

CHAPTER FOURTEEN

Abby stirred uneasily in her bed. The night was half over, but she'd barely gotten any sleep. She could not forget the disgusted look on Sloane's face when he had accused her of being a drug dealer. Then her mind would shift immediately to the feel of his lips against hers. He had just been using her! There'd been no feeling behind it at all. That must be why he'd been assigned to this job, so he could seduce her. He had just been trying to get information from her.

She resolutely tried to shut out the vivid recollection of their lovemaking, but he had left a burning imprint on her. A sensation of intense sadness and desolation swept over her. It was pointless to deny her passion for him, just as it was useless to hope that her burning need for him would ever be satisfied. He had made his contempt for her quite plain, and how could she ever face him again, knowing what he thought of her?

Impatiently Abby pulled her drifting thoughts

together. Why should she care if the police wanted to waste their time investigating her? She knew she wasn't involved with drugs. The harder she tried to ignore the truth, though, the more it reverberated in her head. She didn't really care if the police thought she was a criminal. What hurt was that Sloane believed she was.

Her thoughts raced dangerously in her head. Someone was setting her up. But who? She replayed in her mind every word that she and Sloane had ever spoken to each other. Now that she knew the truth about him, she could see a pattern to his endless questions about Joe and Ned. Now there was a thought! Abby seized on her stepbrother for a moment. He knew more about this than he was telling her. But she couldn't believe that Ned would set her up. True, she'd not had much use for him in the past few years, but it still just didn't fit the Ned she knew. It had to be someone else.

Abby shook her head groggily. None of this made sense. She squirmed in her bed, trying in vain to find a more comfortable position when she heard a noise from outside her room. Abby stiffened and strained her ears. There it was again. Someone was in her home, moving softly through the hall, so softly she could barely hear the feather-like footsteps. She listened, trying to hear where they were going, and clutched the satin sheets to her chest as the footsteps paused outside the door of her room. They stood for a long, agonizing moment, and then creaked past her room toward Adam's room.

Without thinking Abby sprang from her bed. Her fingers closed around the heavy wooden baseball bat that she kept propped in a corner, and she padded noiselessly in her bare feet to Adam's room. A dim, shadowy figure bent over her son's bed. Sheer black fright swept through her. Without hesitation, Abby raised her baseball bat high over her head and swung it downward with a satisfying crack. The figure slumped noiselessly to the ground.

Abby gingerly stepped over the would-be kidnapper and bent over her son, quickly reassuring herself that he was sleeping soundly, oblivious to the disturbance. Then she turned her attention to the intruder, automatically grasping for a pulse. He was still alive. Straining her muscles, she tugged him over onto his back to get a better look at him. In the darkness it was hard to see, but she caught a glimpse of a bulbous nose dominating a meaty face. It was the same man whom she had caught watching her house, who had thrust the money into her hands. Somehow she was not surprised.

Suddenly a thick hand was clasped firmly over her mouth and a low voice growled in her ear. "Make one move, and the kids gets it. Understand?"

Abby froze and then nodded. She could feel something sharp sticking her in the ribs-- a knife. Her captor dragged her to her feet and pulled her out of the room through the living room and into the kitchen where she was shoved down onto a chair. The light was flicked on and she glared defiantly up at the unshaven, snaggle-toothed man who stood grinning down at her. "Well, now. What have we here? An unexpected bonus!"

Abby shivered under his gaze. "What do you want?" she asked, hoping her voice sounded calm and steady.

"Now, we just dropped by for a friendly visit. We thought we'd take you and your little boy for a nice little ride."

The menace in his voice sent chills racing down Abby's spine. Icy fear twisted around her heart. She swallowed with difficulty. "Who are you? Why are you doing this?" she demanded. If she could keep him talking, maybe she could find a chance to get away.

The face loomed closer to hers. "You'll find out everything you need to know soon enough. Now you just come along with me real nice and quiet and everything will be fine."

His hand clamped firmly around her upper arm, yanking her from her seat. With an outraged cry, Abby pushed ineffectually at him with her hands. "My, you're a fighter aren't you?" he grinned. "That's okay! That's how I like it!" His knife flickered in his other hand and he held it against her throat. "Now you'll go into the bedroom and pick up your little boy. You'll carry him to the car and not make a sound. Understand?"

Abby bit her lip and nodded. Fear like she'd never known before welled up inside her. The man jabbed at her neck with the knife.

"Move!" he ordered. With an inward sob, Abby forced her legs to move. Then, without warning, her knees buckled. As she stumbled, she sensed a momentary release in his grip around her arm, and sharply smacked the side of her hand against his wrist, forcing him to release the knife. Quick as a flash, she kicked the weapon out of reach. With a howl of rage, her assailant smacked her savagely on the side of the face and threw her to the floor.

Suddenly he was lifted straight up into the air and flung onto the floor beside her. Sloane Jameson towered over him, and when he tried to rise, Sloane knocked him out with a firm fist to the jaw. Then he turned to Abby. "Are you all right?" There was a spark of some indefinable emotion in his eyes.

Abby ignored his proffered hand and scrambled to her feet, gingerly running her fingers alongside her jaw where the man had hit her. "Yeah, I'm fine." Her voice quavered and she coughed to clear her throat. "There's another one in the bedroom."

Sloane's mouth spread into a thin-lipped smile. "I already took care of him," he said succinctly. "If he comes to, he'll find he's handcuffed to your front door."

Abby managed a shaky smile. "I'd better call the police."

"You forget who I am," Sloane said in a queer tone. "Squad car's on its way."

Suddenly Abby's knees felt very shaky and she sat down abruptly on the chair. "Where did you come from?" she asked. Her stomach was still clenched tight, and she didn't think her pulse would ever stop racing.

"I was awakened by a loud thunk coming over the speaker." Amusement flickered in the eyes that met hers. "I assume that's when you hit the other guy with your baseball bat. I found it on the floor beside him."

Abby raised her chin with a cool stare in his direction. "I should have realized you had my house bugged," she said bitterly. She knew she should be grateful to him for coming to her rescue, but her feelings of anger and resentment toward him ran too deep. She rubbed the back of her hands over her eyes. They ached with weariness, her jaw hurt, and more than anything, she wanted Sloane to go away and leave her alone.

Sloane ignored her. "When I heard his buddy's voice, I thought it didn't sound very friendly, so I came over to see what was happening." He didn't tell her that when he'd heard the man attack her, he'd been overcome by a blind fury, that he'd been terrified that the man would hurt her before he could get there.

"Thank you. I appreciate it." Abby spoke stiffly, irked by his aloof manner.

"It wasn't for you," Sloane said quickly, his tone coolly disapproving. "But Adam's a good kid. He doesn't deserve to be mixed up in your dirty business."

Tears blinded Abby's eyes. "Adam! They were going to take Adam!" She began to shake as the fearful images built in her mind.

"I'm telling you, lady, you're playing a dangerous game!" The expression on his face was taut and derisive.

"But I'm not!" Abby cried, flinging her arms out in despair. "What will it take to convince you that I don't have anything to do with this!"

"You can't. I've seen too much evidence the other way. The force of his seething reply caught Abby off guard. She pointedly turned her head, refusing to meet his gaze. They sat in hostile silence, avoiding each other's eyes till the police came. The officers were deferential to Sloane, but their manner toward Abby was strictly speculative. "We need you to come down to the station, Ms. Tarleton, to make out a complaint."

Abby passed a hand over her eyes. "Now?" she asked in a strained voice.

Sloane shot her a keen glance. Her face was pale and pinched, and her eyes were ringed with black circles. Her swollen jaw throbbed an angry shade of red, and somehow he sensed that if she tried to stand, her legs would buckle beneath her. "I'll bring her to the station in the morning," he said with gruff authority. "She can file charges then. That is," he turned his gaze skeptically to Abby, "if she plans to."

"Of course I do," Abby snapped, pushing her hair out of her face with the back of her hand.

The policeman looked from her to Sloane and back again. With a smirk, he touched the brim of his cap and went to the kitchen to help his partner. The man on the floor in the kitchen was starting to come around as the policeman pulled him to his feet. He glowered at Abby. "Better watch out, Miss Tarleton," he drawled. "If you don't come to the Boss, he'll come to you. He don't like the way you've been jerking him around."

Sloane nodded in satisfaction and looked straight at Abby. She looked stunned.

After the men had been loaded into the police car,

Sloane turned back to Abby, his face a stony mask. "So, you've been jerking the boss around, have you?"

Abby raised her head, assuming all the dignity she could muster. "I don't know what he was talking about," she replied in a low, tormented voice. "But I don't suppose it would do you any good to tell you that."

"No, it wouldn't." Suddenly Sloane reached out and touched the side of her jaw. Abby steeled herself for his touch, but it was surprisingly tender. "It's swollen," he said. "Let's take care of it." He grabbed a dishtowel and filled it with ice. "Here."

Abby took it and held it to her cheek. "Thanks," she said grudgingly, not wanting to be beholden to him for anything. She felt the heat stealing to her face as Sloane gave her body a raking gaze. "I must look a mess," she said, tremulously.

"No, you don't." Sloane's voice was as soft and thick as honey.

Abby looked down and for the first time became aware that she was wearing only her nightgown, a gray satin shift that fell loosely from her shoulders where the straps were knotted together. No wonder that police officer had been giving her the eye. Sloane leaned a hip against the counter, his gaze dropping boldly form her eyes to her shoulders to her breasts. The smoldering fire she saw in his eyes and the answering flame that burned deep within her took her aback. Her pulse throbbed at the base of her neck, and her entire body felt heavy and warm. She cleared her throat and tried to pretend she was not affected. "I mustn't keep you up," she said, raising her eyebrows in a gesture of dismissal. "Thank you for coming over, but I'm sure that you don't need to stay."

Sloane shook his head, his eyes still admiring her beauty. "What about Adam?" he asked with quiet emphasis.

The question stabbed at her heart. "What about him?"

"Don't you think they'll try again?"

Her hand flew to her mouth. "Oh no! Please no!"

Sloane came close, looking down at her cynically. "I can arrange to have him taken to a safe place, if you'll agree. He'll be well taken care of." He held his breath, waiting for her reply.

Hope sprang into Abby's eyes, to be quickly replaced by suspicion. "Can I go with him?" she asked.

"If you turn state's evidence." Sloane's gaze bore down into hers with an almost imperceptible note of pleading.

Abby's face filled with despair. "But I don't know anything!"

Sloane's face hardened. "Then it's just Adam." He spoke so viciously that she wondered how she could ever have thought him kind.

With a moan of distress, she turned away. "All right!" she said in a voice torn straight from her heart. "Just please, keep him safe."

"Why don't you go get him ready? I'll make some phone calls." Now his voice, so angry just seconds before, was infinitely compassionate.

Abby first went into her room and pulled on her blue robe. Then she crept into Adam's room and quickly packed a small suitcase. She filled a cloth bag with his favorite airplanes and stuffed animals. By the time Sloane came to the door with a tall, friendly-looking woman, Abby was ready. "Adam," she said quietly.

The little boy was instantly awake. "Mommy has to go away for a few days. You're going to stay with this lady while I'm gone. I'll be back soon." Abby controlled her voice carefully, not wanting her son to pick up on her inner turmoil.

The woman smiled at Adam. "Hello, Adam. I'm Nancy. Will you come with me?"

The little boy groggily rubbed his eyes, then nodded. Nancy bent down and he put his arms trustingly around her neck. Abby and Sloane followed them to the car, Sloane carrying Adam's bags. He put a comforting arm around Abby as the car pulled away. "He'll be all right. I promise," Sloane said. He gave her shoulder a reassuring squeeze.

Abby swallowed hard. "I should be with him."

"It's your choice."

Abby lurched away from him and turned to go back into the house. Sloane halted her escape with an iron grip around her wrist. He pulled her to him, his eyes blazing down at her with glittering fury. "Abby-"

"Oh, go away! You wouldn't believe anything I said anyway!" Abby shook her wrist but could not dislodge his hand.

Sloane rocked back on his heels. "Try me," he challenged.

Abby searched his face suspiciously. He remained impassive under her scrutiny. "Look, I don't know what this evidence is that you've supposedly got on me. But you aren't even giving me a chance to explain my side of it. I don't have anything to do with this business! How can I convince you of that?"

Sloane sighed. "You can't. I've seen it too many times. High and mighty people like you, always swearing up and down that they have nothing to do with drugs. But there they are, up to their necks in it. My brother was the last person in the world you would expect to turn to drugs.

He was a fitness freak, Mr. Health Nut Incarnate. Even when we were small, he wouldn't touch anything he thought was bad for his body. He drove my mother nuts by insisting on a vegetarian diet when he was five."

Sloane's eyes stared into the distance as he spoke. His voice dropped to a tortured whisper. "I knew something was wrong. I felt it in my gut, right here." He punctuated his words with a fierce jab at his stomach. "But I didn't do anything about it. I just couldn't believe it." Sloane’s broad shoulders heaved in giant, ragged breaths. "He died! My brother died, because I refused to believe that he could be involved in something as sordid as drugs!"

Abby touched his cheeks, the skin hot beneath her fingertips. "I'm sorry, Sloane. About your brother."

Sloane's pain carved merciless lines on his face. "I found him, you know," he rasped, unaware of her touch. "Found him in his bed. He was cold, so cold. I called him, but he didn't answer me." A muscle throbbed in his jaw as the words plunged from his throat. At last he looked at her with icy, unforgiving eyes. "You don't know what it feels like to be responsible for the death of someone you love!"

Abby's eyes met his with the shock of understanding. "Oh don't I? If I hadn't married Joe, my stepfather would probably still be alive. It wasn't just Ned who broke his heart. It was me. The knowledge that I married a man who was involved with drugs brought on his fatal heart attack. I've had to live with that for every day of my life." Her lips trembled and tears glistened in her eyes.

Sloane roused from his daze and lightly fingered a loose tendril of hair on her cheek. "Hey, you can't blame yourself for what Joe did."

"Why not? You're blaming me for it." Abby's eyes looking back at him were large and guileless.

Sloane winced. "Ouch! One corner of his mouth twisted upward. Dipping his head slightly, he said, "All right, Abby. I'm willing to be convinced. I'll present my evidence, and listen to your side."

Abby smiled a lopsided smile. "Over coffee?"

"Of course. I didn't get much sleep last night," Sloane said, looking wryly at the sun as it peeked over the horizon.

They both became aware that they were still standing on the sidewalk in front of the duplex, Abby in her robe and Sloane in the worn shorts and ragged shirt he had thrown on when he heard the strange noises from Abby's house.

Sloane studied her pensively. The rosy glow from the sun highlighted the contours of her face, and her hair blew gently in the early morning breeze. She held out her hand to him. "Come on, Sloane."

He looked at her outstretched fingers, then clasped his hand over hers. "All right," he agreed, giving her fingers a soft squeeze. "Let's go."

CHAPTER FIFTEEN

Abby's face softened as she entered the living room carrying a tray of coffee and donuts. Sloane leaned back in the recliner, eyes closed, his chest rising and falling evenly. Gently she set the tray down on the coffee table and curled up on the sofa, tucking her feet beneath her legs. Sloane's eyes flickered, and he looked abashed. "I'm sorry. Didn't mean to fall asleep on you."

"It's okay. I know we're both tired." Abby indicated the tray. "I found some donuts in a box in the cupboard. Coffee's good and hot." She waited till he picked out a donut and then looked at him firmly. "Okay. Now, tell me why you decided to start spying on me."

Sloane had the grace to look embarrassed. "It started with Joe." He fell silent, organizing his thoughts in his head. As he did so, he realized that nothing between them had really changed. Their moment of shared revelation out on the street did nothing to alter the fact that he still had a job to do, and right now that job required him to find the evidence that proved Abby guilty. He picked up a doughnut from the plate in front of him and took a bite, sending her a piercing look as he chewed. He was curious to see how she would handle herself. "It started with the letters Joe wrote to you from prison. The censors forwarded them to our office. Of course, we found them most interesting." He looked at her challengingly.

Abby raised her shoulders in a dismissive shrug and returned his gaze without flinching. "Did you? I never read them. They're all in a box in my closet."

"I know," Sloane said with satisfaction. "I found them when I searched your house."

A pink tinge crept over Abby's face, but she smiled smoothly. "Then you also know that those letters are still sealed. "I never read them. I'm just saving them for Adam's sake."

Sloane was momentarily shaken. Quickly his mind flashed back to his hurried search of Abby's closet. His own face flushed as he remembered how he'd been more interested in Abby's clothes than in the box of letters he had found. He'd barely looked at them, but now that he thought about it, he couldn't remember any signs that they had been opened. But, he told himself quickly, he couldn't remember that they had been sealed either. Her words meant nothing.

With quiet assurance, he continued, "When Joe got his early release we-"

The heavy lashes that shadowed Abby's face flew up and she half rose from her seat. "Joe's out of prison?"

Sloane's expression held a note of mockery. "You didn't know?" His tone clearly indicated that he didn't believe her.

"No. I didn't." Abby set her coffee mug firmly down on the table beside her for emphasis. "He's not been around here."

"Yeah, right," Sloane muttered in a voice heavy with sarcasm. Then he remembered that Abby had not been present at the meeting between Ned, Joe, and L.C. in the duplex the other evening, that there was, in fact, no evidence of any contact between Joe and Abby.

Abby's lips puckered with annoyance. "So, you're telling me that you've been assuming for quite a while that I'm involved in his drug ring?"

"Of course. The letters clearly indicate that you took over for your husband when he was arrested."

"Joe's letters say that?" Abby leaned forward in her seat, her head shaking in puzzlement. A note of excitement crept into her voice. "Sloane!" she clutched the arm of the couch. "Joe must be the person setting me up!"

"So you say," Sloane said, raising his head with a

disdainful sneer. "We have more than letters as evidence."

"Oh? Such as?" She regarded him with impassive coldness.

"Well, for instance, the payoff you took a couple of days ago right on the street outside this house."

Abby stared at him, totally baffled. Then, to Sloane's surprise, she burst out laughing. "So that's what that was! Sloane, that guy had been following me around for days. I finally went over to tell him to buzz off, and he just shoved the money at me and drove away. At first I thought it had something to do with Ned, but once I found out he didn't know anything about it, I took the money to the police."

Sloane weighed her words with a critical squint. "I can check that out, you know," he said, with a silken thread of warning in his voice.

"You do that," Abby shot back, challenging him with her eyes and voice. "The sooner the better."

Sloane shifted in his chair before continuing. "And how about all those drug orders you keep getting over the phone?"

Abby ran her fingers through her hair and looked exasperatedly around the room before resting her gaze on his face. "You know, this is all beginning to make sense. I had no idea what those calls were about. I thought some business had accidentally given my number out as theirs."

She leaned forward, her voice dropping as she took on an urgent tone. "Check with the phone company. I complained about those calls and arranged to have a new number. An unlisted one." She paused to let the words sink in.

Sloane moved over to where Abby sat, looming over her, trying to intimidate her into making some slip that would quell the confusion rising inside him. "What about the fact that every place you fly to just happens to be one where this drug ring has a dealer. If there's no dealer in the place, you don't fly there."

Abby's mouth dropped open and her eyes widened in mock horror. "That's evidence?" she asked, her voice lined with sustained laughter.

Sloane's eyes narrowed as he continued to drive his points home. "We also have a piece of paper that Connie found on your counter. It has a list of dealers that we've arrested lately."

Abby's eyebrows shot up, and she spoke in a voice heavy with sarcasm. "And, of course, I suppose you checked to make sure it's in my handwriting, and that my fingerprints are on it."

"Well, no," Sloane admitted, his composure visibly under attack. Quickly he changed to a different line of evidence. "But what about those last minute packages you fly out for Bob's boss?"

"He works for a printing company!" Abby's voice dripped with scorn.

"That's just a cover. He's a member of the drug ring."

Abby shook her head, rejecting his evidence. "None of this is proof. It's all circumstantial. Any two-bit lawyer could tear your case apart."

Sloane bent his head slightly forward. "I'd say the comment of that goon just now was pretty damning, wouldn't you?" He lowered his voice. "See, a lot of what I do is based on gut thinking. I get a feeling in my guts, and I act on it."

Abby stood up, forcing him to take a step backwards, and looked him squarely in the eye. "And what do your guts tell you about me, Sloane Jameson?"

Sloane lowered his gaze. That was just it. Inside, everything he had was screaming that this woman could not possibly be involved in the drug ring, that she was a victim just as she said. He took a half step toward her, but controlled the urge to reach out and sweep her into his arms. Determinedly, he pushed his feeling aside. "You're in it, lady. And I won't rest till I see you rotting in jail along with your brother."

Abby sighed, too tired to argue with him any longer. "Fine. I guess we have nothing more to say to each other then." She turned away and swallowed a yawn. "You can do what you want. I'm going to bed. There are still a few hours before civilized people are up." Without giving him a second glance, she padded out of the room.

Sloane stared after her. More than anything, he wanted to run after her. He wished he could believe her, but how could he? It had been drilled into him from his earliest days at the academy, where there's smoke, there's fire, and there was definitely a lot of smoke around Abby Tarleton.

He sank back into his chair and pounded his fist into his hand. The woman twisted his mind so much that he no longer knew which way was up. He had to wrap the case up soon or he would go out of his mind. With a deep sense of conviction, Sloane resolved that he would stick to Abby like glue until he had the evidence he needed to put her behind bars. That was his last coherent thought before drifting of into sleep.

Sloane heard a soft noise and opened his eyes to find himself staring straight into the barrel of a gun. His eyes traveled upward and met the menacing glint of a small, swarthy man. "Take it easy, copper," the man said in a softly accented voice. "I don't mind using this."

Sloane looked toward the bedroom. He should never have let Abby out of his sight. She must have phoned for reinforcements.

Someone grabbed his hands roughly from behind. Sloane instinctively tried to turn around, but the man with the gun shook his head warningly. Resignedly Sloane stared straight ahead as his hands were tied tightly behind his back.

There was a nose from the back of the house, and a blonde man with a neatly trimmed beard and mustache came out, pushing Abby none too gently in front of him. She had changed into a pink, sleeveless blouse and a tan pair of shorts, and to Sloane's intense amazement, her hands were tied behind her back like his. He studied her face, frowning at the fear her saw therein. The man with the gun motioned to Sloane. "On your feet, cop. Someone wants to see you."

"I told you, you were playing with dangerous people, Abby," Sloane drawled lazily.

"Say another word and I'll shoot," the dark man warned in a cold, expressionless voice. "Now get up."

Sloane rose unsteadily to his feet. "Aren't you afraid someone will see us?" he said, ignoring the man's words.

"Not really," the man returned, grinning. "And even if they do, they won't think anything of it. Now come on." He pocketed the gun, but kept his hand in his pocket, the look on his face leaving no doubt that he would draw the gun out at the least sign of resistance.

Abby and Sloane were hustled down the sidewalk to a waiting, dark blue mini-van, and were pushed inside to the middle seat. Sloane kept watch out of the corner of his eye for someone he could appeal to for help, but Abby lived on a quiet street and there was no one in evidence. Abby and Sloane sat in the van, shoulder-to-shoulder, knee-to-knee. Behind them sat the man with the gun, which he kept pointed at Sloane's head. The blonde, mustachioed man slid into the driver's seat while the third man sat in the front and turned to keep a gun pointed at Abby. Sloane was able to get a good look at the third man for the first time. The man was huge, the stereotypical thug. An ex-boxer, Sloane decided, judging by his crooked nose and crinkled ear.

"I don't suppose it would do any good to ask where we are going?" Sloane asked, with an effort managing to keep his voice light.

"You'll find out soon enough," the driver growled.

Sloane wondered how long they would keep up the masquerade of kidnapping Abby. "You can go ahead and untie her, you know," he said airily. "I know all about her."

One of the men raised his eyebrows. "You do?"

"What was in the coffee, Abby? Something to knock me out?"

Abby flashed him a disdainful look and pointedly turned away from him. The men laughed.

Sloane continued. "Of course, Abby, now I have the evidence I need. And you'll be put away for a long time. Kidnapping a police officer is a serious crime." That was the last thing Sloane was able to say. The thug behind him raised his gun and brought it crashing down on Sloane's head.

“What did you do that for?" Abby cried as Sloane slumped against her shoulder. She struggled to turn to look at him. His eyes were closed, his face pale and glistening. She tugged at the bonds holding her hands, but they were tight, much too tight.

The man in the seat behind them laughed a sinister, mocking laugh. "I don't like uppity cops," he said, reaching into his pocket for a plug of tobacco that he bit off and chewed vigorously on one side of his mouth. "And I don't like uppity broads. So just shut your yap, and enjoy the ride."

Abby adjusted her position, trying to get more comfortable, but there wasn't any way to manage it. Sloane's weight was heavy against her, and she looked down worriedly at his black, unruly hair. She hoped he wasn't badly hurt; she had a feeling she was going to need his help. Even though he hated her and thought she was a criminal, she didn't want to face whatever she was about to face on her own.

Sloane's eyes fluttered open. His brow wrinkled as he tried to remember where he was. His cheek was resting against something soft and curved. He turned his head a fraction of an inch, caught sight of Abby's swan-like neck and realized he was leaning against her chest. His memory flooded back to him, and he tried to lift his head, but the movement sent waves of nausea through him. At his moan, Abby turned her pale, oval face down to look at him. "Are you okay?" she asked in a voice that trembled slightly.

“What do you care?" Sloane asked brutally. He saw the sudden hurt in her eyes at his words, and guilt flickered at the edges of his mind, but he recklessly pushed it aside.

Abby licked her lips. "You probably have a bump on the back of your head. He hit you pretty hard."

"No kidding," Sloane said sarcastically. "How long have I been out, anyway?"

"Perhaps an hour."

With a great effort, Sloane managed to lift his head and look around. He cast an eye at their captors. The man in the passenger seat in the front stared morosely ahead, smoking a cigarette, while the man in the back seat was half asleep. Sloane looked out the window, trying to gauge where they might be. He recognized the low hills west of Fort Worth. The countryside was filled with barbed wire fences, tall grass, and short, twisted mesquite trees. With a grimace of pain, he turned back to Abby. "How long are you going to keep up this charade?" he asked in a voice loaded with ridicule.

Abby rolled her eyes. "Get real! If I'd engineered this, I certainly wouldn't have allowed them to make me sit right next to you."

Sloane grinned and moved himself even closer to her. "I was just thinking that was mighty nice of them," he said with a leer.

"And I wouldn't have let them tie my hands so gosh darned tight. I haven't had any circulation in my fingers for hours."

Sloane grunted to let her know he had no sympathy for her. Then, unbelievably, he felt a feather-light touch at his hands. Holding his breath, he strained to move over, and felt her fingers working at his bonds. "Serves you right," he said gruffly as he felt the rope loosen. Luxuriantly he stretched his hands behind him and stifled a gasp as he felt the blood rushing back to his fingers. The man in front turned to look at them. Sloane caught his breath and sullenly returned the glare. The man nodded his head in satisfaction and turned away. Sloane could feel Abby relax almost imperceptibly beside him.

Abby and Sloane exchanged cautious glances. Her eyes were filled with pleading and trust, while his were dark with suspicion mixed with hope. With their eyes, they formed an uneasy alliance. He was still not entirely sure he trusted her, but for the moment he didn't have any choice. He reached for her hands and started working on her bonds.

Now both of their hands were free. He caught Abby looking at the guy in the passenger seat and shook his head just a fraction of an inch. They would have to wait till they go to wherever they were going. Then they could make their move. Sloane leaned his head back and kept an eye out the window, trying to keep track of where they were. The van kept carefully to the back roads, and there were few indications of their location.

In his head, Sloane carried on a pitched battle with himself. Before long, the car would arrive at wherever they were going, and it would be time to make his move. The question was, could he trust Abby or not? At least two of the men had guns, and he wouldn't be surprised to find the driver carried a gun too. And there was no telling what kind of manpower there was where they were going. He didn't like the odds, but if he could depend on Abby, his chances were a little better. She had untied his hands, and her hands had been tied tightly, he'd give her that. She definitely was a prisoner, but if push came to shove, would she help him, or would she sell him out to save her own skin? And the fact that she was a prisoner certainly didn't mean she was innocent. Not by a long shot. If she had tried to cross the Boss, he would no doubt react exactly like this. If Sloane trusted her, he would be putting his life in her hands, and all the evidence, all his training, screamed against doing that.

Sloane gnawed at his lower lip. A voice hammered in his head, one he'd wrestled with ever since this assignment began. One part of him said Abby wasn't guilty; that someone was setting her up, and another part of him dismissed this reaction as pure sentiment. Sloane sighed, no closer to a solution. Either way, he was putting his life at risk. The choice he had to make was between his own gut feeling, and the cold, hard evidence.

It was mid afternoon before the van turned into a long, gravel driveway that wound its way between small, rolling hills before ending outside a rambling, two-story brick house. It was surrounded by a wooden rail fence that outlined a green, neatly manicured lawn.

Bushes lined the front of the house, and there was a small grove of pecan trees to the side. No one was in sight.

Abby had been asleep on Sloane's shoulder. Now she roused herself and sent him a questioning look. Sloane nodded infinitesimally. Abby's fingers reached for his, and she gave his hand a squeeze. A smile touched Sloane's lips.

The man in the front got out of the car and opened their door, motioning them out with his gun. "Okay you two. Out!" The swarthy man in back, now wide awake, kept his gun trained on them.

Abby made as if to stand and gasped. "I don't think I can move. My legs are killing me."

"Yeah, right sister. Move it!"

Abby rose slowly. With a lightning fast movement, Sloane struck at the man behind them, sending his gun flying through the air. At the same time, Abby sprang from the van and knocked the other man's gun to the ground. Quick as a flash, she ran toward some bushes for cover, with Sloane close behind her. They could hear the men swearing behind them, and looking back, they saw that they had recovered their guns and were charging after the fugitives. A bullet whizzed past Abby's head, and she ducked, none too soon.

"Come on!" Sloane yelled. He shot out of the bush, legs pumping furiously. Abby dashed after him, her heart in her throat. Bullets whizzed past their heads as they ran for the fence. Sloane vaulted over neatly and turned to help her scramble over. Then they continued running till they were in the thickest part of the pecan grove. They both leaned against a tree, gasping for air.

Abby bent forward with her hands on her knees, her chest heaving up and down as she tried to catch her breath. "Where are they?" she asked when she could speak again.

Sloane peeked out from behind his tree. "They've fanned out to look for us. I don't think they saw us enter the grove."

"What do we do now?" Abby asked, her heart thudding rapidly in her chest.

Sloane scanned the scene, his mind rapidly running through the options. "If we can get back to the van, we can use it to escape! Let's circle back around behind the house and come up from the other side. And pray they don't have dogs."

Abby nodded. Keeping close together, they darted from tree to tree till they were at the fence again. They climbed over and, staying low to the ground, ran from bush to rock to mesquite tree. With neither cloud nor breeze to offer relief from the heat, they were both drenched in sweat. They swung wide around the house, moving as fast as possible, but it still took time for them to go all the way around to the back.

They paused under a scraggly pine bush to rest, both

panting heavily. Sloane made a sudden motion with his hand, and Abby followed his line of sight. One of their abductors was stalking in their direction. Sloane and Abby hunched under their bush, trying not to make a sound. They huddled so closely together that Abby could feel Sloane's muscles tense as the man approached. His footsteps clumped nearer and nearer till he was about fifteen feet away. Abby concentrated on not moving a muscle. The footsteps topped, and Abby was convinced he had seen them. A cold knot formed in the pit of her stomach as for one agonizing moment, she waited for the crack of the gun. Then a shout summoned the man back to the car, and with a grunt, he retreated. Abby and Sloane both exhaled huge sighs of relief.

As soon as they thought it was safe, they scurried out from under the bush and continued around to the other side of the house, where they flattened themselves against the wall. Sloane stuck his head around the corner and nodded with satisfaction. "Good. They're not in sight. I think they went down the driveway to keep us from getting to the road. Let's get to the van while we have a chance."

They ran for the vehicle, adrenaline surging through their bodies. Sloane opened the driver's side door. "Damn! He took the keys! You sit behind the wheel and keep watch! I'll see if I can get it going. As soon as you hear the motor, be ready to take off!"

Abby slung herself up behind the wheel and turned her head, scanning the trees and bushes beside the house for the men. "They're in the grove beside the house," she reported, her heart in her throat. She squinted against the sunlight, then her fingers tightened around the steering wheel. "Hurry! They've seen us!"

With a roar, the motor came to life. Sloane ran to jump in the car. At the same time a shot rang out and Sloane fell to the ground beside the car. "Go!" he screamed. "Abby! Get out of here!"

Abby didn't hesitate. She leapt out of the car and ran around the front of the car, her feet scrabbling for a footing on the slippery ground. She flung Sloane's arm around her shoulder and helped him rise to his feet. "Come on! Let's get in the van!" she urged.

With her arm around him, Sloane was able to struggle to the door of the car. Abby yanked it open and Sloane, although dizzy with pain, managed to climb inside. Abby slammed the door and raced to the driver's side, but she was too late. The three men ran up to the van, panting heavily, dripping with sweat. The bearded man gripped Abby's arm and twisted it behind her back, causing her to gasp with pain. She saw Sloane look from her to the steering wheel. "He's going to leave me," she thought, her heart lurching in despair.

The short, swarthy man motioned at Sloane. "All right, folks. No more games. Get out of there."

Face tight with pain, Sloane opened the door and fell more than climbed out of the van. Abby, her eyes enormous pools of emerald green shining in her pale face, made a moan of protest and tried to go to his aid, but the big man held her back, twisting her arm until she thought he would tear it of.

Sloane's hand was clapped to his shoulder with blood oozing out from beneath his fingers. His whole upper body burned like fire. He and Abby exchanged looks, and then resignedly he turned toward the house.

They moved inside and were hustled to a room down a shadowy hall. The bearded man opened a door and motioned them to go in. "Get in there!" he grunted.

"What about him?" demanded Abby. "He's hurt!"

"Serves him right!" The man laughed a sadistic laugh that sent shivers down Abby's spine. Then he slammed the door, leaving Abby and Sloane alone in the darkness of their prison.

CHAPTER SIXTEEN

Abby caught Sloane as he slumped toward the carpeted floor. She lowered his body gently and tugged at his shirt. Fortunately it was old, and the material tore easily. Taking the fabric firmly between her hands, she gave it a good jerk and ripped it off his shoulder. She drew a quick, inward breath at the blood oozing from the ugly, gaping wound at the top of his arm. She squinted to take a closer look. "I think it actually just grazed the skin," she said finally. "It doesn't look like the bullet is still in there."

Sloane tried to turn his head, but she stopped him with a firm hand on his forehead. "Quit squirming!" she ordered. "You're making it worse."

"You stayed for me." Sloane pinched his eyebrows together in puzzlement.

"Of course I did," Abby said as she tore a wide strip from the bottom of her blouse. Lips set determinedly, she wound the pink cloth around Sloane's shoulder, then leaned on it with her hands to try to staunch the bleeding.

"Why?" Sloane worried at the question like a dog with a bone.

Abby shot him a queer look. "I'm just an idiot, I guess." A tinge of exasperation coated her voice. She shifted her hand slightly and grunted with satisfaction when she saw that the bleeding had stopped. "I've got to elevate this wound," she muttered under her breath and looked around the room for something appropriate. Her eye lit on a floral-patterned sofa in the corner. Crossing to it, Abby snatched one of the cushions and tucked it under his shoulder with dexterous hands.

Sloane's eyes flickered. "Abby?"

"I'm here. You're going to be all right," Abby said with a confidence she wished she felt.

"You should have gone!" Sloane mumbled. His eyes seized on her face and clung to it like a beacon at sea.

"I couldn't leave you here to face them by yourself!" Abby said fiercely. Her hand, feather-light, closed around his wrist to feel his pulse. He reached out, lacing her fingers with his own, clinging to the warmth of her skin.

"It's cold," he said faintly before he drifted off.

Abby took a deep breath, struggling to keep her fragile self-control. "He's going into shock! I don't dare elevate his feet though," she thought, remembering that he had been hit on the head with a gun. "That might make him worse. I've got to keep him warm somehow!" She surveyed the room again and saw a couch, a wooden rocking chair, plush blue carpet and bared window, but nothing that would act as a blanket. Not knowing what else to do, she tugged the remaining cushions off the couch and laid them beside Sloane on one side. Then she stretched out beside him on the other side. She molded her body to his, and wrapped her arms around him, sharing her warmth with him. The sunlight faded as together they lay in the darkened room. Abby's eyes were as wide as a frightened rabbit's as she tried to assess the situation, but her mind kept returning to the horrible moment when she'd heard the shot ring out and seen Sloane fall. For an endless, terrifying instant, she'd thought he was dead, and with an awakening clarity that left her reeling, she knew that she could not bear it if anything were to happen to him.

She rested her head on Sloane's uninjured shoulder and listened to his breathing. It was even and steady, reassuring her that he was okay. Weariness enveloped her as she tried to concentrate on figuring a way out of the mess they were in. She finally drifted into wisps of sleep, rousing frequently to check on Sloane's condition. Each time, he was sleeping soundly.

When she woke up completely, several hours later,

the house was silent. Either the three kidnappers had left, or they were asleep. It was dark outside, but a pale moon shone through the room's barred window. She looked at Sloane and found his clear blue eyes studying her with a curious intensity. His good arm was wrapped snugly around her, holding her tightly against him. Abby lifted her head and checked his bandage. It was still snug and secure, with no sign of fresh bleeding.

She pushed a wayward strand of dark hair off his forehead. "How do you feel?" she asked in a voice, which, with an effort, she was able to keep calm and detached.

Abby looked away. "I would have done the same for anybody," she insisted.

"But you did it for me." Sloane's voice was soft, compelling. He reached his good hand up and trailed down the side of her cheek. "After the way I treated you...you should have gone off and left me."

Abby's heart lurched into her throat and she blinked hard, smothering a sob. "I thought you were dead!" The words tumbled out of her mouth, unbidden.

Now there was an almost hopeful glint in his eye. "Would you care? The words were spoken so softly that she might have been imagining them, but she could see in his eyes that she wasn't.

As tears slowly rolled down her cheeks, glistening in

the soft, shimmering light from the moon, Abby admitted, "Yes, I would."

"Why?" Sloane's voice traced the path of the tears down her face.

The words caught in Abby's throat. "Because I love you." Her voice broke in dismay. She cleared her throat and repeated the words. "I love you. I know you hate me, and that you never want to see me again, but I can't help it."

A smile found its way through the mask of uncertainty on Sloane's face and he struggled to sit up. Suddenly, with a clarity that had eluded him before, he saw the truth of the matter. He had been wrong about Abby. She was a victim just as his brother had been a victim. Suddenly it no longer mattered that she had been Joe Tarleton's wife. All that mattered was that she loved him, and he loved her.

"What are you doing? You've got to lay still!" Abby pressed her hands ineffectually against his chest.

"It's okay. I'm fine. I've just got to sit up," Sloane said in a voice that brooked no argument.

"Why?" Abby demanded, still trying to push him down.

Putting his good hand to her waist, he drew her to him. "Because," he whispered, his breath hot against her ear. "I want to be holding you like this when I tell you that I love you too."

Abby drew her breath in sharply; then she relaxed. She sank into his cushioning embrace, discovering that her head fit perfectly between his neck and his shoulder. "I'm not hurting you, am I?" she asked as they rocked gently back and forth.

"Oh no," Sloane said as his hand explored the hollows of her back.

The reality of their situation suddenly struck Abby and she lifted her head. "Sloane, we shouldn't be doing this. We've got to find a way out of here!"

"Is there any way out of this room?" Sloane asked, dropping the whisper into her hair.

"Not that I've found. But I was busy taking care of you." Abby disengaged herself and pushed herself to a standing position. With hands on hips, she turned to survey the room. "The window has bars," she said, half to herself. "But still..." She stifled a protest as Sloane rose to his feet.

"It's okay," Sloane reassured her. "The bullet just grazed it, remember?" He crossed to the window and examined it closely. Abby noted that for all his bravado, he didn't use his left arm at all but let it dangle at his side. Finally he turned, discouraged. "No help there," he scowled.

Abby turned toward the door. "This is the only other way out. I wonder if we could break through."

With one long stride, Sloane was at her side.

"Perhaps," he said uncertainly. "But our friends out there no doubt would hear us."

Abby shivered, crossing her arms over her chest and rubbing her upper arms. "They certainly have the air conditioning turned up high enough," she remarked.

Sloane looked ruefully down at his own bare chest and shorts, then back to her clad in her shorts and cotton shirt that ended just below her breasts since she had torn off the bottom to wrap his shoulder. "Neither one of us is really dressed for this," he said.

"What's going to happen to us?" Abby asked, her stomach churning with fear and frustration.

She could see the struggle in Sloane's face as he tried to decide whether or not to lie to her. An almost imperceptible shake of his head said it all. Dropping his good arm around her shoulders, he spoke softly. "It doesn't look good. This gang is not likely to let us go. Since they've put us in here instead of killing us right off the bat, they must have something in mind for us. Whatever it is, I doubt we'll like it."

Abby leaned into his embrace and let her head drop onto his good shoulder. "What about your people? Won't they notice that we're gone?"

"Eventually." Sloane buried his hand in her hair, twining it around his callused fingers, then relaxing it. "But they won't have any idea where we are."

Abby raised her head to look at him. "This just can't be it! What about Adam? I'll never see him again! I'll-" She stopped and bowed her head, biting her lips to keep the tears inside.

"I'm sorry," Sloane whispered in a broken voice. "This is my fault. If I had only believed you! I should have sent you into protective custody with Adam."

Abby shushed him with a hand to his lips. "Shh! You mustn't blame yourself. You were doing what you thought was right." She forced a laugh. "I probably would have done the same thing, considering."

Sloane chewed on his lip as his thoughts spun rapidly in his head. "You know, someone sure went to a lot of trouble to set you up."

"It has to be Joe," Abby said flatly.

Sloane stroked his chin and regarded her thoughtfully. "But why would Joe want to incriminate you?"

Abby bent her head and studied her hands. "I don't know. Maybe to get revenge for me divorcing him. But one thing's for sure. If it is Joe, he'll be coming around sooner or later to gloat." Her expression darkened with an unreadable emotion, and Sloane felt a terrible tension in her body.

His good arm tightened around her. "I'm sorry,

Abby." He shook his head fiercely. "Damn! Why didn't I listen to myself?"

Abby blinked with bafflement. "You mean you thought I was innocent."

"Yeah," Sloane said, hiding his eyes from her. "But Connie kept railing at me for getting personally involved with you. Every time I tried to suggest that you might be innocent, she threw the evidence back in my face."

Abby snorted. "Some evidence!"

"Yeah, well, Connie and I are partners. One of the reasons we work so well together is we keep each other in line. Only this time I should have been keeping her in line." Sloane's eyes clung to hers, pleading for forgiveness.

Abby's thoughts turned to a different line of inquiry. "Did I hear you say she was married?" she asked slowly with a twinge of envy.

"Oh yes. Been happily married for years."

Abby raised her head and jutted her chin out. "And how does her husband feel about you?"

Sloane's mouth twitched with amusement. "Oh, we're great friends." Laughter bubbled from his throat. "Abby, I could never go for Connie. She's not my type."

"Oh?" Abby wavered.

"Absolutely. For one thing, she's much too short. I like my women tall." His eyes dropped down to her long, slender legs. "And her hair is brown." His voice, deep and sensual, sent a ripple of awareness through her. "I've never cared much for brunettes." He reached out and touched her blonde hair lightly. "And Connie hates kids," he added with a note of satisfied finality. "While I love them."

Abby sat perfectly still as Sloane lowered his head and tenderly kissed her mouth. "You see," he said huskily, trailing a finger sensuously along the curve of her lips. Connie's not my type at all."

Abby's eyes shone bright in the pale light from the window. She could feel his heart thudding against her own, could feel the tingle of excitement building within her. She reached up with her hand and traced the coarse outline of his unshaven cheeks.

Sloane's voice came in ragged gasps. "Abby, I need you."

Abby drew a shaky breath and let it out slowly. Her face turned upward, and he pressed his lips to hers, caressing her mouth more than kissing it. Her blood throbbed with passion, and she returned his kiss hungrily, entwining her arms around his neck. Her trembling limbs clung to him, never wanting to let him go.

They fell asleep wrapped in each other's arms. Abby woke up several hours later to find Sloane's eyes regarding her with a tender smile.

They could hear noises from outside the room. The hum of a radio, a door opening and closing, footsteps moving around. Sloane caught Abby's fingers with his and raised them to his mouth for soft kisses. "Our friends are up."

"Well, I wish they'd bring us something to eat," Abby said, rubbing her bare stomach.

Sloane started to say something, but was interrupted by a new noise of in the distance. "What is that?" he asked.

Abby's eyes widened. "It's a plane! Single engine! And I think it's landing here!"

Sloane sent her a measuring look. "If we could get to that plane, could you fly it?"

Abby nodded with assurance. "But how can we get out of here?"

“I'm not sure yet. Just keep your eyes and ears open, and follow my lead. We probably won't have time to talk about it before we make a break for it. But I do know one thing, if we get a chance; it will be the only one we get.

frustration but the only way out was past the man with the gun, and that posed too great a risk. Especially since he heavily suspected that Joe and the Boss were also armed.

The Boss turned wide, questioning eyes on Sloane. "But why not? It would make Joe so happy, and I find that it really pays to keep my employees happy as much as possible."

Abby glanced warily at Sloane, afraid of what he might do. She swallowed with difficulty and forced the words from her mouth. "Go ahead, Sloane. Joe and I do have a lot to talk about."

Sloane caught the merest flicker of her eye and nodded reluctantly. "All right. Let's go."

Sloane followed the Boss down a tiled hallway to a lushly furnished, sunken living room, his eyes straining to hear what was happening in the room between Joe and Abby, but he could hear nothing.

The Boss glanced sideways at Sloane and patted him on his injured arm. Sloane caught a groan in his throat. "To what do I owe the honor of this invitation?" he said between clenched teeth.

The Boss led the way into the spacious, mirror-walled living room. "Drinks, Jorge," he ordered graciously.

Wordlessly Jorge pocketed the gun in his shoulder holster and went behind the bar. The Boss waited until he was given his drink, then he raised his eyes questioningly at Sloane who shook his head.

"No? Pity?" The Boss drained his drink in one gulp and then turned back to Sloane. "I had you brought here because you really are getting rather tiresome. It was fun watching you waste your time on Mrs. Tarleton for a while, but enough is enough."

"You did set her up," Sloane stated with cold satisfaction. He suppressed an inward leap of joy at this confirmation of Abby's innocence. If only he had trusted her. If he ever got out of this mess, he vowed, he would make it up to her.

"Oh yes. It was Joe's idea. It really was very naughty of her to divorce the poor boy when he was in prison and couldn't defend himself." The Boss shook his head sadly. "Now, however, it's time for us to move on to other things. But before we kill you, I did want a chance to chat with you."

Sloane lowered himself on the velvet plush covered couch and looked interested. "Oh, so you are going to kill me?"

"But of course. We can't let you continue to operate. It's very bad for business, you know."

"Like you killed Connie?"

The Boss laughed a nasal, high-pitched laugh. "Not

yet. But we will get around to her. Right now she's busy investigating a hot tip down on the border. One that will turn out to be a wild goose chase, of course. Oh, it's such fun to play games with the police."

They were interrupted by a noise from the doorway. Joe was standing there with his arm around Abby who looked up at him adoringly. Sloane's heart flip-flopped at the sight of her. "We're going out to check the plane," Joe announced.

"Have you worked things out?" The Boss raised his eyebrows.

Abby trailed a hand lovingly over Joe's face. "Joe knows I've always loved him," she cooed. "But I thought he'd be in prison for years. If I'd known he was getting out so soon, I never would have filed for divorce."

Sloane hid a grin as Joe shot him a triumphant look. "I told you Abby was mine," Joe gloated.

The Boss smiled in satisfaction. "Such a lovely couple," he murmured as Joe and Abby, entwined lovingly, left the house.

"You said you were going to kill me?" Sloane said in a hard voice.

"Oh yes. But first, of course, I need you to tell me the names of the other agents in your department."

"Go to hell," Sloane said politely.

The Boss's eyes narrowed. "Oh dear. That really isn't very nice. We do have, you know, most unpleasant ways of making you talk."

Jorge moved idly from the bar to a position directly to Sloane's right. Sloane lifted his head suddenly and looked out the window as if he heard a noise. As he had hoped, Jorge's eyes lid to the side for just a second, long enough for Sloane to leap to his feet and knock the gun out of Jorge's hand. The two men fell to the floor in a jumbled heap, both of them vying for possession of the gun.

Jorge, his eyes glittering madly, aimed his blows at Sloane's injured left shoulder. Sloane deflected the blows with his right hand and tried to land some good ones on his opponent. Inch by inch, they rolled nearer to the gun until it was within reach. Jorge placed his hands firmly on Sloane's shoulders and held him to the floor. Sloane gasped with pain and instinctively lifted his knee. Jorge doubled over from the force of the blow. With a mighty heave, Sloane thrust the other man off of him and stretched his fingers out until they clasped around the barrel of the gun. He pulled it toward him, and as Jorge made one final lunge, Sloane fired.

Jorge collapsed in a dead weight upon Sloane's body. Sloane shoved him off and bent over him. The bearded man was dead. Sloane's shoulder was bleeding again. He swayed dangerously, dizzy from the fight and from the loss of blood. The room swirled around him and for an awful moment, he thought he was going to collapse. Then the room righted and he regained control of himself. He stepped behind the bar, and found a towel, which he clasped to his shoulder, pressing it in under the bandage as best he could. There was no sign of the Boss or of the other two men who, along with Jorge had abducted them from the duplex.

A cold knot formed in the pit of Sloane's stomach as he thought of Abby out there somewhere, alone with Joe and the boss. "I've got to get to her!" he said aloud.

With the gun held warily in his hand, he stepped out through the sliding glass doors onto a covered patio. He crept stealthily around the side of the house, his ears pricked for any noise. He scanned the area beyond the house and caught a glimmer of metallic green behind the trees in the pecan grove. "That must be the plane," he muttered. His eyes darted furiously around. No one was in sight, so he took a chance and sprinted to the pecan grove. He bit his lip as he looked at the surrounding the trees. He'd have to climb between the bars; no way was he going to be able to jump over it with his injured shoulder. He rammed the gun into the pocket of his shorts and clambered through the fence as quickly as he could, scraping his back on the wood, aware of how very vulnerable he was at that moment.

Once on the other side, he slipped from tree to tree till he could see a mowed field. Keeping to the shelter of the grove, he moved closer till he could clearly see the plane.

A body was stretched out under the wind of the plane. Sloane recognized Joe, and with a squint saw a large metal wrench on the grass nearby. His eyes traveled to the cockpit of the plane and his heart caught in his throat. Abby was climbing into the plane, while behind her, gun glinting in his hand, stood the Boss.

Abby climbed into the plane, conscious all the while of the Boss's gun pointed at her head. She wondered bleakly where Sloane was. She had heard the gun go off in the house and knew that with Sloane's injured shoulder, he couldn't have held out for long against the blonde man. She shuddered inwardly at the thought and pressed her hand convulsively over her face as she stumbled into the pilot's seat.

"Drop it right there!"

Abby's heart leaped into her throat. It was Sloane! She whipped around. He stood directly behind the Boss, his gun pointed firmly at the Boss's head. The bald man's grip tightened on the gun that was pointed at Abby. "I will shoot her," the Boss warned in a squeaky voice.

Abby saw the skin around Sloane's lips tighten, but his voice sounded steady. "Then I will shoot you."

For a long, terrifying moment they were locked in the scene. Then the Boss lowered his gun. Abby let out a long, slow breath.

"Throw it outside the plane," Sloane directed. His voice, though quiet, had an ominous quality.

With a murderous look, the Boss complied.

"Now come out, with your hands up." Slowly the Boss swung himself out of the plane. Sloane kept the gun trained on him. “Abby, would you be good enough to pick up his gun?"

Abby started to clamber out of the plane, but froze as a new sound assaulted her ears. The Boss looked up with a malevolent grin on his face. "I'd say this changes things a little, wouldn't you?" he taunted gleefully as two Land Rovers skidded into the driveway in unison. From the look on Sloane's face, Abby could tell that this was not the cavalry riding to the rescue.

The Boss's words unleashed something in Abby. "Sloane!" she cried in a low, urgent tone. "Get in the plane! Now!"

Without hesitation, Sloane climbed up behind her, keeping the gun trained on the Boss. "Okay, Abby, let 'er rip!" he directed tersely.

Abby started the engine and hoped that Joe had taken good care of the plane because she sure didn't have time to preflight and check it now. Glancing quickly at the instrument panel, Abby saw that while they were low on fuel, there should be enough to get them to Meacham Field in Fort Worth.

"Come on, Abby! Move it!" shouted Sloane above the roar of the engine. Abby looked back and saw that both cars had skidded out of the driveway onto the grass and were almost upon them. She quickly pulled on the throttle to increase power to the engine and let up on the brake. The plane moved hesitatingly.

Shots rang out. With a terrifying screech, the bullets tore through the skin of the airplane. Abby checked hurriedly, but nothing important seemed to have been hit. As the plane slowly picked up speed, Abby looked out her window and was alarmed to see the long grass bending in the same direction they were headed. They were taking off with the wind instead of against it!

Abby swore loudly, pounding her fist in frustration against the door panel beside her.

"What's wrong?" shouted Sloane, the noise of the

engine all but drowning out his voice.

"We're taking off with the wind at our backs. Means it's going to take us longer to get off the ground." Abby gritted her teeth in frustration.

One of the Land Rovers pulled even with Abby's left wing, guns looming ominously out of its windows, bullets splattering everywhere.

Abby and Sloane ducked as the window on that side exploded, spewing slivers of glass throughout the plane. Abby turned the plane to the left and forced the car to drop back. She then quickly veered to the right so the second car couldn't creep up on them.

The noise from the engine and rushing air whooshed deafeningly through the shattered window and tiny shards of glass tinkled in Abby's hair. Every time she moved her head, a chorus of them showered to the floor of the plane. "Are you okay?" she yelled at Sloane, turning her head to give him a quick once over as the plane continued to gather speed. He had suffered a couple of scratches on his face from the glass but otherwise looked fine.

"I'm all right!" Sloane peered out the windows at the cars still racing beside them. "But if you don't get us off the ground soon, they'll shoot this plane to shreds!"

Up ahead, Abby saw that they would soon run out of the smooth, grassy runway. Beyond that there was nothing but rocks, trees and holes. "How close are they?" she yelled back at Sloane.

"What did you say?" Sloane leaned forward, but Abby waved him off.

Never mind, she thought. Not enough time for an answer anyway. She quickly let up on the throttle, hit the brake, and turned the plane to the right. Both cars shot past her, guns still blazing. The car on the right passed under her wing, just missing the body of the plane, and had to swerve to miss the propeller. Abby smiled grimly and pulled back on the throttle to send the plane speeding down the runway again back the other way. This time she had plenty of space and the wind against her. She should be up in the air and out of sight before the goons could catch up.

The cars squealed as they turned around and sped closer to the plane, shooting at it continuously. Then the plane lurched into the sky, and as the distance between the ground and plane grew, so did Abby's elation.

Without warning the plane slipped to the left in a sudden descent. "Blast it, Sloane!" yelped Abby. "I think they shot some of the control cables." She wrestled with the controls, sweat beading on her forehead until finally she had the aircraft steady and level at six hundred feet.

"Sloane?" she asked, suddenly realizing he'd not replied to her last outcry. "Sloane?" She spared a glance behind her. Sloane sat with his head slumped to the side, body sagging against his harness.

Abby was horrified to see blood oozing from a new wound on his right shoulder. "Sloane!" Abby screamed as she turned further around. The plane again slipped and descended rapidly. Swearing under her breath, Abby once again fought for and regained control of the aircraft.

"Stay calm, Abby," she muttered to herself. "I saw his chest move so he's still alive. Just call on the radio to Meacham Field control tower and they can have an ambulance there waiting for us."

She reached for the radio, then halted in dismay, her hand hovering in mid air as she stared at the two neat bullet holes in the radio. "Oh no!" she groaned. Then, mustering all her strength and ability, she spoke pleadingly, "Hang on, Sloane, hang on! We're almost home free. Just hang on, please!"

Through the mist in her eyes she flew on to Meacham Field, anticipating one of the worst landings she had ever made. At this point, she didn't care. She just wanted to get Sloane to safety.

At last she saw the familiar landmarks of the airfield and circled, looking for a clear runway. She knew the tower was probably trying frantically to contact her, but without the radio, she'd just have to go in without their say so. She couldn't stay in the air for much longer; she didn't have enough fuel left in the tank.

She skimmed over the runway, every muscle in her body tensed in the effort to control her disabled plane. She bounced once, and one of the landing struts broke with a sickening crack. Then the plane careened down the runway on its belly, metal screeching against the concrete, coming to a rest, finally at the far end.

Abby didn't waste a second. As soon as the plane stopped moving, she sprang from her seat and tugged at Sloane's limp body, wanting to get him well away from the bullet-riddled aircraft.

A crowd gathered quickly and helped her lay Sloane on the soft grass nearby. Someone tried to pull her away, but she shook him off, determined to stay as close to Sloane as possible. She sat beside him, fingers clasped tightly around his, till the ambulance came. Then she was escorted to the main office of the airport to face what she knew would be an endless round of questions. The last sight she had of Sloane was of his deathly pale body being lifted into the back of the ambulance before it roared away.

CHAPTER EIGHTEEN

Abby waited until the judge swept from the chambers before she approached the broad mahogany table where her brother sat. Mr. Hestler, standing beside Ned, busily stuffed papers into his brief case, looking quite pleased with himself, while a uniformed police officer stood beside the table waiting to take Ned away. "It really went quite well," Mr. Hestler gloated, fussily pushing his wire-rimmed glasses up on his nose. "Much better than I expected."

"Eighteen months, Ned," Abby said in a deflated voice.

Ned shrugged. "Could have been much worse. And it's minimum security, Abs. Seem plush compared to most of the places I've lived."

"Oh, the judge was quite reasonable," Mr. Hestler broke in. "Of course, with Ned agreeing to testify against the other members of the gang, the judge really couldn't do any less."

Abby managed a wry smile. "Thank you, Mr. Hestler, for all your help."

"Always a pleasure, you know. I mean, er..." The little man appeared even more flustered than usual. Abby and Ned exchanged conspiratorial smiles. He really was a good lawyer, but just seemed overwhelmed when dealing with anything other than legal matters.

Brother and sister watched as he gathered his things and blundered out of the courtroom. Ned sat back and crossed his arms over his chest. "So, Abs, what do you hear from your drug agent friend?"

A pale, pink flush washed over Abby's face, but she kept her voice expressionless, not letting on how much the question stabbed at her heart. "Sloane? Nothing, actually. I don't expect to."

Ned sent her a knowing glance. "Funny. I kind of got the impression he was sweet on you."

Abby managed a laugh that she didn't feel. "Oh, that was just an act. He was trying to seduce me so I'd confess to all my nefarious activities." She was saved from further questions by the police officer who tapped Ned on the shoulder.

"Time to go, Ned."

Ned stood up and awkwardly wrapped Abby in his arms. "Write to me, Sis."

Abby hid her face in his shoulder, not wanting him to see her tears. "I will, Ned," she said in a muffled voice. She looked up and placed her hands over his cheeks, turning his head downward. "When you get out, you'll have a place to stay."

Ned nodded, unable to speak. He dropped a hurried kiss on her cheek and then turned, holding his hands out for the policeman to lock the handcuffs on.

Tears blurred Abby's vision as Ned was led away. Blindly she left the building and got in her car. With Ned gone, she felt strangely bereft. She'd often wished he would go away and stop bothering her, but now that he was gone, she knew she would miss him.

She drove home on autopilot, all the events of the past few weeks replaying themselves in vivid detail in her mind. Ned had pleaded guilty to the charges against him, and agreed to testify against the other members of the drug ring. Abby had initially felt betrayed when she learned that Ned was one of the people who had helped frame her, but she readily forgave him when she saw his heart-wrenching remorse. The whole episode seemed to be a turning point for him, and he had resolved with a fervor Abby knew was genuine to put his life back on an even keel once he was out of prison.

Joe, the Boss, and the other members of the drug

ring had been arrested and were being held without bail until their trial. The police were optimistic that they would all be put away for a long time.

All of which left only one loose end. Sloane. She had not seen him since that day he had been loaded into the ambulance and taken away. After interminable hours of questioning by first the airport authorities and then the police, she had staggered home to find a brief message from Sloane on her answering machine. Her knees had buckled with relief when she had heard his voice, weak, but alive, reassuring her that he was fine, and would be in touch with her as soon as possible. Since then, she'd heard nothing.

Abby's hands clenched around the steering wheel. She had tried to get Sloane out of her mind by throwing herself into her work. She accepted all the flights she was offered and tried to let the boundless joy she felt while flying satisfy the gnawing hunger she felt inside her, but it wasn't working. No matter what she did, his face lingered in the black stillness of her thoughts.

It was probably all just part of a day's work to him she told herself philosophically. Seduce the beautiful woman, get what you need from her, and leave her standing on the tarmac. Never mind if you took her heart with you when you left.

Abby called the police once to ask when Sloane and

Connie's furniture would be moved from the duplex, but it seemed that Sloane and Connie worked for separate government agency, and the local police did not know anything about them. Abby wasn't concerned about the rent money; she had already received a check for the remainder of the time left on the lease, but she just didn't like having half of the house vacant, to say nothing of the fact that every time she looked over at the drawn curtains, she was reminded of Sloane.

She parked in front of her house and paused before turning off the ignition. Her body stiffened. A moving van was parked in front of the duplex, and the sidewalk was full of men carrying things from the house to the van. Abby's heart caught in her throat at the sight of the tall, wide-shouldered man standing in the front lawn watching the movers. His head swiveled to look at her as she stepped out of the car, and he sent her a devastating smile. Abby felt a warm glow flow through her as she crossed over the lawn to stand next to him.

"Hello." His voice was as deep and resonant as she remembered.

"Hello." Abby managed a tremulous smile. "How have you been?"

Sloane lifted an eyebrow at her polite tone. "Fine. And you?"

Abby tossed her head. "I've been fine."

"Good." Sloane reached out an arm to drop around her shoulder, but she neatly sidestepped the embrace.

"What about your wounds?" she asked, still affecting a nonchalant air.

Sloane grinned broadly. "Got to keep the bullets as souvenirs. Now I have matching stripes on each side. But," he raised his eyebrows and sent her a jesting look. "They both work just fine." He raised and lowered his shoulders as proof.

Abby bit her lip to hide a smile. "And how is Connie?" she continued perfunctorily, snipping the words off her tongue.

There was a pale blue flash of laughter in Sloane's eyes. "She's fine. She came home sputtering with fire about the wild goose chase she'd been on. Seems she took off to tail someone and ended up spending three days chasing him around the Big Bend wilderness, unable to get word to any of us. Cell phones don't work out there, you know. She was more than a little disgusted to learn we'd wrapped up the case without her help." Sloane's eyes darted around the yard. "Where's Adam?" he asked.

"He's at the sitter's. I decided to come home and change before picking him up." Abby sent a disgruntled look down at her court clothes, a conservative dress, high heels, and worst of all, panty hose.

Sloane's mouth twitched with suppressed merriment. He turned his attention back to the movers, carefully scrutinizing their actions. "Hey, be careful with that!" he yelled as one of them dropped a box. "That stuff is fragile!"

Abby tried not to let his casual attitude bother her, but she simply couldn't let him go without finding out why he hadn't been in touch with her. The words hung on he lips till she finally blurted them out. "Where have you been the past couple of weeks?"

For some reason, Sloane seemed to find her anger amusing. "As soon as I got them to let me out of the hospital, I had to finish doing my job out in the field. Wrapping up loose ends. That's what my kind of work is all about." He bowed his head and looked searchingly at her. Sometimes I'm away for months at a time and my family and friends can't contact me."

"Oh." Abby was taken aback by his words. It certainly wasn't what she had expected. "That must be hard for- for Connie, being married and all."

"Her husband knew the score when he married her." Sloane's eyes looked far away, his lips pursed thoughtfully.

"I don't think I could handle that," Abby said forthrightly. "I need more stability. A pilot's life is crazy enough as it is."

"I kind of thought you'd feel that way," Sloane said, his countenance immobile.

Abby felt an instant's squeezing hurt. She continued, struggling to keep the passion out of her voice. "It's not just that. I couldn't live not knowing whether I'd ever see my husband again. I couldn't live knowing that there are people like the Boss out there who want his blood. I just couldn't live like that." Abby shook her head firmly.

Sloane turned and faced her squarely. Without warning, his hand closed over her shoulder. "I know. I couldn't live like that either. That's why I've never married."

Abby nodded to show she understood. As she switched her gaze toward the men carrying furniture out of the duplex, Sloane reached into his pocket and held out a key chain. He dropped the keys into Abby's hand. Then he held his hand out, palm up.

Abby stared at him in dazed confusion. Her sea mist colored eyes sought his questioningly. "What-"

"The keys to your place."

Her mouth dropped open. "I just told you! I can't live like that!"

"Neither can I," Sloane agreed easily. "That's why I'm quitting field work. I've taken a desk job."

"You?"

"Yes." Sloane hesitated; then the words tumbled over each other in their haste to get out of his mouth. "I meant what I said, Abby. I love you. When I think of how I nearly lost you..." He closed his eyes to hide the pain, and then lowered his head. "I want to marry you, live with you, love you forever. Please say yes." His voice ended on a pleading note as he searched her face hopefully.

Abby turned away and bit her lip, the soft light of joy washing over her.

"Abby?" Sloane put his hand on her shoulder.

With a muffled laugh, Abby turned and flung her arms around his neck. "Yes! Yes! Yes!"

They clung to each other, laughing and kissing with delight. Then, hand in hand, they walked into Abby's side of the duplex.

THE END

Printed in the United States
53743LVS00005B/1-102